BECOMING LITTLE LEXIE:

A DADDY DOM ROMANCE

SUE LYNDON

Becoming Little Lexie: A Daddy Dom Romance
Copyright © 2014 by Sue Lyndon

Contact: suelyndon@suelyndon.com

Cover design by Angela Haddon
www.angelahaddon.com

Published in the United States of America
Sue Lyndon
www.suelyndon.com

CHAPTER 1

As Alexa attempted to sit up in bed, all the muscles in her body protested and a piercing pain shot through her chest, reminding her of her broken rib. She gasped and closed her eyes until the agony faded, cursing her injuries. Footsteps approached from down the hall, and she knew it was William bringing her lunch. The kindness flickering in his eyes when he paused in the doorway made her want to cry. She took a deep breath and forced a smile, not wanting him to think she didn't appreciate all he'd done for her since the car accident a week ago.

"There's my beautiful girl."

The appetizing aroma of tortilla soup entered the room with William. Her stomach rumbled as if on cue, but she ignored her hunger and gazed at him, marveling at how untiringly nurturing he'd been to her. Though appreciative that he was taking such good care of her, the warmth and longing his constant care aroused deep down struck her with worry. Desires she'd never expected to experience battled to surface, and she kept pushing them down in hopes that they would fade away. But every time William walked through their bedroom door with that handsome smile of his, she felt like a little girl inside, a little girl who longed for her daddy's loving reassurance that everything was going to be okay.

William placed the tray of food on the nightstand, sank down next to her, and began petting her hair. His touch lifted her out of her troublesome thoughts. Endorphins kicked in as he gently drew his fingers through her locks, and she was filled with adoration as she gazed up at her handsome husband of two years. Sadness fell upon her a moment later, and she blinked rapidly and hoped to hold her tears at bay. She normally didn't cry easily, but she'd been very emotional since the accident.

Without a word, William grabbed a tissue and caught the first tear to roll down her cheek, and all the rest that followed. He always did, and she loved him for it, but guilt filled her as he continued wiping the moisture from her face. She couldn't possibly explain her tears to him. Not in a thousand years.

"You really didn't have to stay home again today, William." Alexa grimaced as another piercing pain stabbed at her chest. She pressed a hand to the wrap that circled her torso, waiting until the worst of the pain passed. "I feel bad that you're wasting all your personal days on me."

William raised an eyebrow at her and clasped her hand. "Young lady, who's the boss around here?" His tone was teasing, but she knew he still expected an answer.

She sighed and grinned through her lingering tears. "You are, sir."

"Now, I happen to love you very much, Alexa, and I intend to stay home with you until I'm certain you can get around safely on your own. I don't want to hear anymore nonsense about me wasting personal days on you. Do you want me to make you keep a punishment journal for when you are all healed up, young lady? Hmm?"

Alexa flushed, and despite her pain, felt a rush of heat travel between her thighs at his threat. She and William practiced domestic discipline in their marriage and he took his role as head of household very seriously. She had no doubt he'd instruct her to start keeping such a journal if she mentioned his personal days again, or if she misbehaved otherwise. "I won't bring it up again." Her cheeks still burned from his scolding.

He stayed with her while she ate lunch, and after she finished he carried the tray from the bedroom, promising to check on her again soon. Her heart panged with sadness and confusion overcame her when the urge to call him 'Daddy' and beg him not to leave yet overcame her for the umpteenth time. She pressed her eyes shut and tried to understand her sudden longing.

After a handful of failed relationships with vanilla partners, Alexa had confessed her needs to her friend, Tina. To her surprise, Tina had given her a knowing smile and introduced her to one of her husband's friends, and Alexa had been smitten with William ever since. She'd been upfront with him about her desires early in their relationship, and he'd been just as upfront with her. Their mutual belief in traditional marriage and domestic discipline had drawn them together.

But did she dare tell him about her sudden interest in age play? Well, he knew she read the occasional age play book, but she'd once told him that it was something she enjoyed reading about and nothing more. Now she tried to remember the exact expression on his face and his tone during this conversation, a conversation they'd had before marriage. She thought she'd seen a twinkle in his eye, but she didn't know what it meant. God, she just wanted the feelings to go away and for life to return to normal.

They had a strong marriage, and she felt guilty for suddenly wanting more from him; she resolved not to bring it up, especially now. She felt bad enough that he'd taken a week of personal time to stay home with her. If he went over his allotted personal days, he'd start losing vacation days. Closing her eyes, she recalled the night of the accident and shuddered.

It had just started to rain, and the road had been slippery. As she drove through an intersection in the middle of town, a truck smashed into the passenger side of her car, totaling it. The elderly man in the truck had been apologetic and claimed he'd thought the light was green. By some miracle, neither Alexa nor the old man had been seriously hurt.

Ever since that night, she'd experienced a shift in her emotions and her desire to be submissive to William. She tried to analyze it, and she thought perhaps the shock of the accident coupled with William's extra attentive care had awakened the little girl inside her. The stress of being laid off from her accounting job a month ago probably contributed to her fragile state too. She grabbed another tissue and dabbed the fresh tears from her face. Or maybe the pain medication was making her completely loopy. She'd tried to go without it, but a broken rib hurt something awful.

She closed her eyes and settled against the pillows stacked behind her, her thoughts spinning a million miles an hour. A naughty thrill always coursed through her when she began a new age play book, and she'd sometimes fantasized about William taking on the role of her daddy and treating her as his little, but it had only been a fantasy. She'd never been unsettled in their marriage and wanting to try something more, until now.

Maybe her need would dissipate after a few days. She could only hope. She just wanted everything to go back to normal. For her to heal and for William to return to work. Then she could resume her job search.

She picked up her e-reader and tried to concentrate on a new book, but it was no use. She'd finish a page only to have no memory of what she'd just read. Sighing, she set the e-reader aside and stared out the window. Sun streamed through the curtains and danced across the floor each time the backyard trees swayed in the breeze. If it hadn't been for the accident, she'd probably be enjoying an afternoon jog in the nice weather. Her insides wouldn't be twisted into knots either.

As she continued to stare out the window, trying not to think about her new desires, and failing miserably, she heard William rattling around in the kitchen. Pots and pans clanged together. Cabinets slammed shut. After a few minutes, the smell of baking cookies drifted upstairs, and her mouth watered. Chocolate chip. Her favorite.

Her face crumpled and she pressed another tissue to her face, taking deep breaths and trying to calm herself. She resolved not to take any more of the pain medication, just in case it was partly to blame for her being upset.

He was her husband. She was supposed to be able to tell him anything. She'd promised to never keep secrets from him, especially those that affected their marriage. But what if he thought age play was too weird? She couldn't bear the thought of his rejection, though she knew even if he wasn't keen on exploring it with her, he'd let her down gently. A gentle rejection was still a rejection though.

By the time he brought her fresh cookies and coffee, she'd calmed down enough that she was no longer on the verge of crying, but the look of concern that transpired on William's face revealed he sensed something was amiss anyway.

"What's wrong, sweetie?" he asked as he placed the plate of cookies on her lap.

Wincing, she sat up straight and hoped the stabbing pain left her chest soon. The doctor had said it would take a few weeks for her rib to heal. She couldn't imagine dealing with this discomfort for another week, let alone several. She met William's dark brown eyes, smiling at the flecks of gold that shimmered in the sunlight. "I've always liked your eyes," she said.

His frown deepened, and those dark eyes she loved became steely. "Your attempt to change the subject won't work. Tell me what's wrong, Alexa." He placed the coffee on the nightstand, sank down on the bed, and squeezed her hand.

She felt trapped and struggled for an appropriate response. She certainly couldn't blurt out the truth. Not now. She hadn't even come to terms with her new desires, and she didn't want to discuss them with William yet. Maybe not ever. She took a deep breath and looked down, but he caught her chin between two fingers and directed her gaze back to his.

"Do not avoid my question, young lady. You're starting to worry me. Tell me what's wrong. Are you in too much pain? Do you want me to call Dr. Stevens?"

She shook her head. "Well, it still hurts badly, but that's not what's wrong." She paused, guilt gnawing at her heart because of the lie that rested on the tip of her tongue. "I don't want to take the pain medicine anymore. I think it's making me emotional. I'd rather deal with an achy rib than feel like crying all the time." Well, it wasn't a total lie. It just wasn't the entire truth. Still, she felt guilty. William never lied to her, and he didn't deserve to be lied to.

He studied her for a moment, the sun glinting off the streaks of gray in his black hair. "We can cut the dosage for your pain medicine in half and see how that goes. If you're not suffering too much, then maybe in a few days we'll wean you completely off it."

"Thank you, William." She smiled, relieved. The tension in her chest lessened, but the guilt remained churning inside her like a poison she'd swallowed. She smiled again and picked up a cookie. "You're the best husband in the world, by the way," she said as she bit into the warm, gooey goodness.

He grinned and tousled her hair, then passed her the coffee. "By the way, I've arranged to work from home next week, so I won't be losing any more personal days."

Swallowing a mouthful of cookie dipped in coffee, she glared up at him, annoyance buzzing through her. "But I won't need you next week! I'll be perfectly fine. William, it's a broken rib, nothing more. If I had a job, I'd be going back to work Monday anyway. Please stop treating me like a child." She almost gasped at her choice of words. *Treating me like a child.* That's what she wanted, wasn't it? To be nurtured by William and have all her needs taken care of? Yet she was pushing him away and wishing the accident had never happened and her new desires hadn't been awakened.

His expression softened and he stroked her hair. "I know you could manage without me next week, but I want to stay home with you, Alexa. After the worry of that night…" His voice trailed off and dark clouds gathered in his eyes. He swallowed hard. "I just don't feel like letting you out of my sight yet. Now, no more arguments, or I will make you keep that punishment journal we talked about, young lady."

Another week. She wondered if she could make it that long without breaking down in front of him and confessing her deep need. She wanted to crawl up on his lap in the rocking chair in the corner of the room and snuggle against his chest while he read her a bedtime story. She wanted to hear him say things like "Daddy loves you, Alexa" and "Time for your bath, little girl" and "Alexa Marie Benson, get your naughty bottom in here right now!"

"Alexa, I expect you to answer me."

Shaken from her daydreaming, she glanced up and felt a pang of warmth between her thighs at the stern look he'd leveled upon her. Though he hadn't asked her a direct question, she knew from experience he expected her to acknowledge his statement. "All right, William. I won't bring it up again."

"Good girl." He kissed her forehead, walked to the doorway, and paused. Turning slightly he asked, "Are you absolutely certain that nothing else is bothering you?"

"Yes, William, I am absolutely certain," she said around a mouthful of cookie.

He departed the bedroom and she placed the cookies and coffee aside, her appetite gone. Not only did she have a big secret she despaired to share with him, but she'd lied to his face after he'd asked a direct question. If he discovered her lie, he'd be disappointed in her and she'd be in big trouble. The kind of trouble that usually resulted in a thoroughly spanked bottom. Despair stabbed at her heart when she imagined his disappointment, and dread rolled through her insides at the thought of a serious punishment spanking.

WILLIAM ATTACHED THE ADVERTISEMENT PROPOSAL to the email he'd just finished writing and pressed the send button. Sighing, he ran a hand through his hair and glanced at the clock. Time to start dinner. After closing down his computer for the day, he moved to stare out the open window, looking at the empty street below as the cool spring air drifted against his face. Thunderclouds gathered in the sky and lightning flashed in the distance. He shut the window and headed out of his home office, intending to check on Alexa before he threw together a lasagna.

He wished she'd tell him what was bothering her, because he couldn't for the life of him figure it out. He'd seen the amount of tissues in the trashcan next to their bed. When he wasn't with her, she cried. It killed him that she was crying in secret and wouldn't lay her burdens on him. He'd tried several times to get her to open up, only for her to claim the pain medication was making her emotional and nothing more.

She was down to taking one pill before bedtime to help her sleep, and she'd gone completely without medication during the last four days. Still, he occasionally found her with red-rimmed eyes, and the tissues kept piling up in the trash can.

Normally Alexa discussed her problems openly and he didn't have to drag the truth out of her. In fact, he couldn't remember a time she'd been melancholy for days while bottling her troubles up. Why now? What could it be?

She'd been fine before the accident. She'd been laid off from her job recently, but she'd been steadily applying for new jobs and had even gone to a few interviews already. Financially, they were fine. His job provided enough income for the both of them, so she couldn't be stressed out about money. Perhaps she was bored. Or lonely. Aside from sitting on the front porch, she hadn't gotten out of the house in over two weeks.

A sudden crack of thunder and rain pattering down on the roof dispelled his thoughts of getting her out of the house for a short evening walk.

He entered the kitchen and paused at the sight that greeted him. Alexa was sprinkling shredded cheese overtop a casserole of some sort. Pleasure lighted her eyes and she was humming happily. She looked up, wiped her hands on her apron, and graced him with a dazzling smile.

William opened his mouth, ready to chastise her for getting out of bed, but then smartly shut it when he realized how happy she looked. Though she moved around the kitchen slowly, she wasn't wincing and grabbing her chest with every little movement anymore. Her rib was healing and she was obviously feeling better. His spirits brightened and he grinned, leaning forward over the island. "I'd planned on making lasagna tonight."

"Well, we're having chicken and veggie casserole tonight. You can make lasagna tomorrow night. But please, do feel free to set the table," she said, smirking.

They enjoyed a pleasant meal in the dining room for the first time since Alexa's accident, and after the storm blew over they sat on the front porch, watching as the moon and stars emerged from behind the lingering clouds.

"If I promise not to take a pill tonight, may I have a glass of wine?" Alexa asked, leaning her head against his shoulder.

"Are you sure you'll be able to sleep without the pill?"

"Yes."

He gazed down at her, tucking a strand of silky chestnut brown hair behind her ear and thanking God the accident hadn't been worse. He kissed her cheek. "One glass. You stay right here and I'll be back."

"Make it a big glass!" she called playfully.

Entering the kitchen, he grabbed a bottle of her favorite red wine and searched for the bottle opener. At least her good mood had lasted throughout the evening, he thought as he poured two glasses. Again, he felt a surge of gratitude that she was recovering quickly from the accident.

He couldn't imagine life without his sweet wife. About two and a half years ago, he'd been about to set up an online dating profile to find a likeminded woman, when his best friend Andy's wife hinted that she might have found the perfect girl for him. He'd been hesitant to meet Alexa and didn't want to endure another failed relationship with a vanilla woman he cared about but couldn't be completely satisfied with for the rest of his life. To his surprise, Alexa had brought domestic discipline up before he had, three short weeks after they began dating. She'd imbibed far too much wine, which she later admitted she'd needed for bravery, before confessing her deep need to find a dominant partner she could submit to, a man who wasn't afraid to take her in hand when she needed it. He smiled as he recalled how red her face had turned when she'd said, "I want to be with a man who will p-punish me when I've broken one of his rules. You know, by s-spanking me." They got married six months later.

He smiled as the memories washed over him.

After he returned to the porch and handed Alexa her wine, she gulped it greedily, as if she were trying to get drunk. He shot her a questioning look, but she simply smiled and shrugged before swallowing down the rest of it. He was glad he hadn't poured her a large glass.

"I have something to tell you," she said, placing her empty glass down on the porch. "It's about what's been bothering me these last few days. Or well, these last two weeks."

William sat his wine down and turned in the rocker, giving her his full attention. Her eyes widened, and the light from a lamp inside the living room bathed her face in a yellow glow, revealing prettily flushed cheeks. She twisted her hands in her lap, and he thought her nervousness made her look adorable. Panic flitted briefly through his heart though as he considered the reason for her nervousness. He vowed to fix whatever was bothering her. "Go on," he said, nodding. "Tell me what's going on, sweetie."

"Ever since the accident, you've been treating me differently. I mean, you've been taking care of me very well. You've been extra tender and extra affectionate, and there are times when I feel like… like…" Her eyes widened further and she clamped her lips together, glancing down at her hands as she continued twisting her fingers together.

William's impatience increased, and he bit back a scolding remark, hoping his calm silence and a gentle hand caressing her thigh would encourage her to continue. Several minutes passed, and finally Alexa sighed and met his eyes once more.

"I am very embarrassed over what I'm trying to

tell you. I don't think there's anything wrong with it, but I worry what you will think of me."

"Alexa, I love you, but you aren't making sense. Please remember that I love you no matter what. The only time I want you to feel embarrassed around me is if I'm doing something especially naughty to you with the intention of embarrassing you." He smiled, hoping to calm her fears.

"All right. Okay. It's like this. When you're taking complete care of me like you've been doing since the accident, I feel… like a little girl. I feel as if you're my daddy. I like it, William. And I want to explore this sort of thing with you, if you're willing."

This sort of thing. She was talking about age play, but in her shyness over the subject she was being evasive and wouldn't actually call it by name. He stared down at her and marveled at his little wife. Desire pulsed through him, tingles racing up his thighs as his balls tensed and his cock twitched. Her confession had caught him by surprise, as did his own arousal. She'd stated early on in their relationship that she had no interest in engaging in age play, and he had never given it more than a fleeting thought over the last two years. Thinking about it now, he was rock hard and aching for Alexa.

"You're talking about age play," he said, wanting to be direct.

She flushed and stammered. "Well, I-I guess. M-maybe."

He leaned closer and took her face in his hands, caressing her cheeks with his thumbs as he gazed into her wide blue eyes. "Alexa, do you have an interest in age play?"

"Y-yes."

"And you started thinking about it after the accident?"

"Yes."

It made sense. He'd coddled her during the last two weeks, even helping her get showered and dressed, and this treatment had triggered her interest in exploring a daddy/little girl dynamic with him. William certainly wasn't opposed to trying. If anything, he was eager to begin. His cock strained in the confines of his jeans, and his heart pumped faster as an image of Alexa dressed in a cute frilly dress flashed in his mind.

"How young do you want to regress, Alexa?"

She half sighed, half whimpered. Again, her face flushed bright red in the lamplight. "I haven't entirely thought it through yet. Not too young. I don't want to wear diapers or have a pacifier or be bottle fed."

"Do you want to call me Daddy?"

Her breath caught and she made a little strangled noise. "Y-yes. Do you think that's weird?"

Mindful of her sore rib, he lifted her carefully into his lap and began moving the rocker forward and backward with one foot pressed to the porch. A surge of protectiveness and love spread through him, and he stared down at Alexa with a gentle smile. "No, Alexa, I don't think that's weird. In fact, I'd like to explore this with you. Thank you for finally telling me what was on your mind."

She stiffened in his hold. "Am I in trouble for not telling you the whole truth about why I was upset last week?" Her voice was small and her eyes apologetic.

William continued to rock Alexa as the night sounds swelled around them. Finally, he replied to her, using his sternest tone. "You told a fib to Daddy last week, didn't you, little girl?"

Again, her breath caught, and a second later she gasped twice as if trying to regulate her breathing. "Yes."

He noticed she hadn't called him Daddy yet, but he didn't want to force her. He wanted to wait until it came naturally. Calling her his little girl felt natural though, and he planned to keep doing so and hoped that in time she'd feel the same ease in addressing him as Daddy. "Daddy isn't happy you told a fib, Alexa. Was the medication really bothering you that much?"

She shrugged. "I don't know. I guess not."

"You should have told the truth right away, no matter how embarrassing it was for you, Alexa. Little girls aren't allowed to keep secrets from their daddies."

She squirmed in his lap, her bottom pressing against his throbbing erection.

"I'm not going to spank you because you're still healing. We're going to have to wait several weeks for that, I'm afraid. However, you're still to be punished for keeping secrets and telling a fib, Alexa. Now I want you to go to the guest bedroom and wait for me."

Her brow furrowed as she regarded him with confusion, but she smartly slipped off his lap and stood up. "Yes, D-daddy." She turned and entered the house, leaving William alone with his thoughts as a cool breeze swept onto the porch.

CHAPTER 2

SHE'D DONE IT. SHE'D ACTUALLY TOLD WILLIAM HER secret, and best of all he hadn't looked at her like she had snakes growing out of her head. Well, she hadn't thought he would, but she still hadn't been sure of his reaction to her confession. He'd called her little girl, and before she'd left the porch she'd finally called him Daddy. After fantasizing about it and aching to explore this dynamic with William, it was happening. Her heart raced with excitement.

As she climbed the steps and approached the guest bedroom, she paused and wondered why he'd asked her to wait for him here. Normally he meted out punishment in their bedroom. Glancing over her shoulder, she listened for the sound of his footsteps. When a few minutes passed and she finally heard the front door opening, she scurried into the guest bedroom and flicked on the light.

The room was sparse, only containing a bed, a nightstand, and one dresser. They hadn't painted or done any decorating in it since moving in shortly after their wedding.

Floorboards creaked in the hallway, signaling William's arrival. Alexa turned as he stepped through the doorway, shutting the door behind him and fixing her with a stern look that made her stomach clench. It was the look he gave her moments before she ended up turned over his knee with her bottom bared. Except he'd said he wouldn't spank her yet. Not until she was completely healed.

He arched an eyebrow at her. "Come here, little girl. You know you were naughty."

Her mouth went dry, and she suddenly forgot how to breathe. Taking slow steps, she approached him with her head slightly bowed, feeling like the naughty little girl he'd said she was. He tipped her chin up and peered directly into her eyes. Her knees wobbled together.

"Yes, Daddy?" she asked, simply because she wanted to try the name on her lips again. Warmth filled her when she said it, a kind of safe warmth that caused her to tingle all over and made her heart swell with love.

"Unfasten your jeans and push them down. Daddy wants to see what kind of panties you're wearing today."

Pleasure quaked in her center as she did as he asked, pushing her jeans down past her hips to reveal the skimpy pink thong she was wearing. Her face heated with shame as he stepped back and his gaze zeroed in on her undergarments, or lack thereof. Disapproval shone in his eyes when he looked up at her.

"Those panties are much too grown up for you, Alexa. Come on, let's get them off." He moved forward and helped her step out of her pants, then removed the offending thong.

She flushed as he tossed the clothing on the floor and immediately knelt so his eyes were level with her pulsing center. Oh no, he'd glimpse her moisture for sure. Shame heated her all over, and she felt the blood rushing to her clit, and the throbbing between her thighs increased. She shuddered when he ran a finger through her intimate folds, discovering the level of her arousal. A groan built in her throat, but she pushed it down and only a whimper escaped.

"Alexa, after your corner time and bottomhole punishment, Daddy is going to shave you all smooth down here."

The room spun. Corner time? Bottomhole punishment? And he wanted to shave her smooth too? She struggled to breathe as her heart pounded faster. William rose to his feet and grasped her by her shoulders, his stare dark and intense.

"Tell Daddy why you're about to be punished."

"I was naughty." Her voice didn't sound like her own, and she felt about two decades younger as she stood under his stern, watchful gaze.

"How were you naughty?" His tone was deep and commanding.

"I kept secrets from you and told a little itty bitty fib. I'm sorry, Daddy."

"That's right, little girl. Now I want you to stand in the corner with your bare bottom on display." He guided her to an empty corner and patted her backside, sending a delightful shiver up her spine.

"Oh Daddy, do I have to stand in the corner?" Alexa wasn't sure what came over her, but she gave a little stomp of her foot and stuck her bottom lip out, feeling sullen despite knowing she'd earned this punishment.

"Alexa Marie, you will not stomp your foot at Daddy. Little girls who have temper tantrums end up with very sore, very well-punished bottoms."

She peered over her shoulder, meeting his reproachful gaze. "Sorry, Daddy."

"Nose in the corner, young lady, until I say otherwise. And stick your bottom out a bit. That's it. Good girl." He patted her backside again, three times, each light contact causing the heated pulses of her arousal to quicken. "I will return shortly. If you move out of position, I promise you will be one very sorry little girl when I'm through with you."

On the heels of a threat that sent moisture trickling down her inner thighs, William left the room, and she heard the floorboards creaking in the hallway as he went… somewhere.

Where was he going?

Excitement bounded within her.

An hour ago, she'd been sick with worry over how to confess her needs to William, and now here she was with her nose in the corner awaiting a bottomhole punishment after being told her thong was much too grownup for her.

She whimpered, staring into the corner as she

wondered what size butt plug he'd bring back. Sometimes when he gave her a punishment spanking, he'd insert a plug into her bottom before paddling her to tears. Even though he wasn't going to spank her today, she was still nervous about taking the plug into her tight hole.

The creaking floorboards announced his return, and she felt exposed as she remained in the corner with her naked bottom sticking out. She sensed his eyes on her and considered his reaction to her confession. He'd been rock hard beneath her as he'd cradled her on the porch. What a fool she'd been to hold her secret desires in for the last two weeks. She'd cried herself silly and made herself sick to her stomach on more than one occasion, and her worries had been unfounded. Or so she hoped.

Apprehension twisted in her tummy. What if William decided he didn't want to explore age play after tonight? Or what if her desire to explore her little side with a firm daddy faded? Or what if she grew tired of his nurturing side or it made her feel suffocated? Oh, what was that saying again? If ifs and buts were candy and nuts…

She couldn't remember the rest, and she tried to shut the worries out.

A hand on her shoulder startled a gasp from her.

"Turn around and come with me, Alexa. Let's get the rest of your punishment over with."

Liquid fear churned through her insides as she turned at his beckoning. The thin, whippy cane he used to correct her most serious offenses dangled from his hand. "But you said you weren't going to spank me." A sense of betrayal burned within her, and she glared at him pointedly to let him know exactly what she thought of his change of heart.

"You can wipe that disrespectful look off your face right now, little girl. I'm not going to spank you. I said I was going to punish your bottomhole, remember?"

He wouldn't. Not with the whippy cane. Where he'd gotten the thing, she wasn't sure. It had appeared in his study one day after she'd tried to cover up a speeding ticket with a couple of little lies. A shudder coursed through her as she recalled what an awful sting it packed, as well as the dreadful whooshing noise it produced the moment before it connected with her flesh.

"Please, Daddy," she said, her face heating as she stared at the terrible implement in his hand.

"You can't do that to my bottomhole. I th-thought you were going to use a plug."

"You thought wrong. Now be a good girl and bend over on the bed." He guided her into position with her palms on the bedspread. "I know it'll be uncomfortable for you to reach back and hold your own bottom cheeks apart with your rib, so I will spread your cheeks apart for you. In the future, however, I will expect you to hold your cheeks apart during this type of punishment, just as I require you to do when I put a plug in your bottomhole."

Despite her fear, the knowledge that this wasn't a onetime occurrence gave her a little thrill. She swallowed hard and heat flooded her face, traveling down her chest to deepen the aching in her pussy. Her nipples were tight, painfully so, and her breath came in ragged puffs as she remained bent over.

"As you are about to find out, Lexie, little girls who fib are dealt with harshly."

Lexie. Her head shot up. Had he really just called her Lexie? She glanced over her shoulder and met his eyes in question. "My name is Alexa, Daddy."

He shook his head and placed a hand on her right bottom cheek, squeezing her mound as he held her gaze. "Alexa is too grownup. I think Lexie suits you much better, little girl. Now please turn around, unless you want to watch as I spread your cheeks apart."

She immediately turned around, jumping in place as he splayed her bottom apart with one hand. Flushing, she tensed as he drew the tip of the cane over her private hole. He'd plugged her bottom before, and he'd even spanked her pussy lips during a punishment, but he'd never punished her in such an embarrassing manner as this. She trembled and closed her eyes, wondering how many times he'd bring the cane down on her delicate flesh.

"I'm going to turn your little pucker an even deeper shade of pink than it already is, Lexie. Twenty quick, light strokes of the cane should do it."

"Daddy, that's too much!"

"Light strokes, Lexie. Not full strokes like I've administered to your bottom cheeks in the past. Now be good and hold still. We're going to begin with the first set of five."

Though she knew it was coming, the first whack of the cane against her tight hole left her gasping. Before she could recover from the surprise, William brought it down four more times in quick succession.

"How are you doing, Lexie? Are you in any pain? Aside from your bottomhole, I mean," he said with a smirk in his voice.

"I'm okay, Daddy," she said, touched that he was pausing to inquire about her rib.

"Good." He tapped at her sore entrance a few times, and she flushed again, knowing he was doing it simply to see her hole clench and unclench with each touch. He did the same thing each time he prepared her for a butt plug. "Next set of five," he announced.

Five strokes, light but still packing enough sting to draw more gasps from her, landed directly over her bottomhole. He repeated the process twice more, inquiring about her pain levels before tapping on her sore entrance and then delivering another set of five strokes of the cane. By the time he finished, the shame produced by this unusual punishment combined with the soreness in such a private place had her on the verge of tears. She sniffled and stood slowly with his assistance.

"Your punishment is over, Lexie," he said, warmth lighting his eyes as he stared down at her. He tossed the cane on the bed and gathered her close, petting her hair as he held her against his chest.

Alexa breathed in his scent, marveling at how little she felt each time he called her Lexie. She liked it. She'd never had a nickname before as her parents and friends had always called her Alexa. Not only did it make her feel little, but it felt like an endearment too, and her heart swelled as she peeked up at him.

"I'm really sorry I lied to you, Daddy."

"I know, little girl, and you are forgiven. Daddy still loves you very much."

Tears of happiness and relief spilled from her eyes, and she hugged him tighter.

Later that evening, William brought her to the bathroom and ordered her to strip naked. As he watched, she removed her clothing, feeling vulnerable and embarrassed over what he was going to do her. He gathered a bottle of shaving cream, a razor, and a washcloth, then drew a shallow bath and helped her into the tub. Trembling, she sat in the water, peering up at him nervously with her thighs clamped together.

"Young lady, you know very well what I'm planning to do, so I suggest you open up those legs."

Heart pounding, she spread open under his

gaze, her senses thrumming with desire and excitement despite her embarrassment. Her nipples tightened and she noticed her chest falling and rising rapidly. She blushed as he sat on the edge of the tub and leaned down, running his fingers through her folds. He made a show of inspecting her mound and cleaning it with the washcloth. Next, he lathered her nether lips up with the shaving cream, taking his time.

"Okay, Lexie, be a good girl and hold still for this part." He picked up the razor and gently began shaving her. "Daddy is going to make you all smooth down here."

She held her breath at first, but soon relaxed as he tended to her mound, removing every last trace of hair. Finally, he rinsed her off and patted her dry, and it took all of Alexa's self-control to keep from moaning as he rubbed the towel against her freshly shaven pussy lips.

During the next week, William had a lot of catching up to do at work, despite having worked from home the week prior. He hated that he had to stay late almost every night, but at least Alexa was feeling much better. She still wore the wrap around her rib, but she hadn't had to take any pain medicine, not since before the night she'd confessed her interest in age play.

He became rock hard each time he remembered the bottomhole punishment he'd given her. They hadn't had much time to explore this kind of dynamic further, but now that another weekend had rolled around, he hoped to enjoy a few of the scenes she'd jotted down in the new journal he'd given her, a small pink notebook he'd instructed her to fill up with her specific desires and fantasies relating to age play.

William turned onto their street and spotted Alexa getting out of her rental car, wearing heels and her usual work clothes—a pencil skirt with a dressy top. He waved and pulled into the driveway, happy to be home with his wife and curious to discover why she was all dressed up. He gathered up his briefcase and stepped out of his car.

"William! William!" She walked toward him with open arms, her heels clicking on the pavement. A brilliant smile lit her face, and sunlight streamed down on her silken hair, which fell in waves around her shoulders. "I got called in for a second interview at HTC today. And guess what? I got the job! It's only part-time for now, but after one of their other accountants retires in three months, it will become full-time."

"Alexa, that's great! Congratulations, sweetie." The smell of her shampoo and a hint of perfume filled his senses as he hugged her. "I'm so proud of you."

She giggled and pulled back, gazing up at him with an unwavering smile. "The office is wonderful. Only a twenty minute drive. I'll have my own office and I'll work Mondays, Tuesdays, and Wednesdays, at least for the next three months anyway."

He grinned and tapped her nose playfully. "You can use your four day weekends to clean the house, iron my shirts, and bake me pies, little woman."

Laughing, she grasped his hand as he led her inside the house. Once William shut the door, he gathered Alexa in his arms and kissed her deeply, moving his hands up and down her back. Heat built in his loins, and he cupped her face as their kiss intensified with their rising passion. "We should celebrate," he murmured against her lips. "Dinner out."

"Sounds great to me," she said, wrapping her arms around him as he trailed kisses down her neck.

They enjoyed a quiet, candlelit dinner at their

favorite French restaurant. Alexa filled him in on the details of her new job, including the coworkers she'd met today in passing. The animated hand gestures she made while speaking testified to her excitement. William was thrilled for her success and happy she'd landed a job at one of her top choices.

On the drive home from the restaurant, he glanced over at her, clearing his throat. "Alexa, I haven't looked in your new journal yet. Have you been writing in it every day?"

She flushed. "Yes, William. I've written something in it every day. Sometimes just a few short thoughts, and other times a longer... um, fantasy."

The stirrings of desire tightened his groin. "Good girl. I want you to bring it to me in my office once we get home."

"Yes, sir."

As they neared home, William noticed Alexa growing increasingly nervous in the passenger seat. She kept fidgeting, twisting her fingers together in her lap, and biting her lip as she cast shy glances his way. His blood heated and his pulse quickened as he wondered what she'd written in her age play journal. He ran a hand through his hair and stared at the road ahead. He'd find out soon enough.

The sun was setting when they arrived home, a

pink glow spilling between the trees and neighboring houses. William parked and opened Alexa's door, taking note of her hand trembling slightly in his. He brushed her hair behind her ears and placed a gentle kiss on her lips, smiling at her as he pulled back.

"I'm nervous about you reading my journal," she said, avoiding his gaze.

He clasped her chin between two fingers, directing her eyes back to his. "I'm your husband, Alexa. I want to know everything about you, and I want to help fulfill your desires."

She sighed and her shoulders slumped. "But I don't want you doing this just to make me happy! Maybe we should just forget all about it." She stepped back and folded her arms across her chest.

Scowling at her, William lifted an eyebrow and pointed at the front door. "In the house, young lady. Right now."

Several packages rested in front of the door, and William gathered them up before ushering her inside. He resolved to prove to her that he wasn't simply indulging her fantasies. Annoyance spread through him as he watched her stomp into the living room. If she didn't calm down soon and watch her temper, she'd end up with a sore little bottom. Except… no. He couldn't spank her yet. Not until her rib was completely healed. She had no trouble doing every day activities and no longer needed his assistance getting dressed, but laying across his knee for a proper spanking could aggravate her injury. He wouldn't risk it, but if she persisted in her naughtiness he'd punish her in another, much more embarrassing way. Swollen hard, his cock pressed against his pants as he imagined caning her bottomhole, or plugging her and making her stand in the corner like a naughty little girl.

William carried the boxes to the kitchen table and returned to the living room. Alexa glared at him, her arms folded across her chest once more. Approaching her, he grasped her shoulders and stared down at her, aching to quell her concerns. "I'm grateful you finally shared your age play interest with me, Alexa, and I truly want to explore it with you. So you need to calm yourself down this instant, young lady. Don't get moody and defensive for no good reason."

"William, I didn't exactly hold back in my journal this week. What if you are repulsed by what I wrote? I can't bear the thought of seeing disgust on your face as you're reading my journal. I should have never brought this up." She shook her head, her eyes growing wide with panic. "Please, just let me throw the stupid journal away."

"Fetch the journal and bring it directly to my office, young lady. You have one minute. If you fail to obey me in this, Alexa, I will cane your bottom-hole again with twice as many strokes as last time." He made a show of glancing at his watch to note the time.

Her eyes widened further and her lips parted. She gaped at him for several seconds before turning to run from the living room, her heels clicking on the floor in tune with her rapid departure. Walking to his office, he entered and flicked on the lamp, then took a seat behind his large mahogany desk. Another chair faced his desk, a chair he'd placed there long ago for the times Alexa ventured in his office to chat with him. This time was different though. This time she was being summoned for a purpose more meaningful than a conversation about the weekly dinner menu, house repairs, or vacation plans.

A light knock on the door sounded just in time.

"Come in," he called, standing up. He gestured to the empty chair facing his desk. "Please close the door and have a seat."

Biting her lip, Alexa hesitated, remaining in the doorway with the pink journal clasped in one hand. William remained on his feet, one hand pointing at the empty chair until she finally closed the door and took a seat, sitting on the edge of the chair as if preparing to run for her life.

"Please hand me your journal, Alexa." Sitting down, he reached across the desk, holding out his hand with his eyebrow raised.

She clutched it to her chest, worry filling her features. An untamed lock of hair fell forward, dangling across her cheek as she avoided his eyes. "I don't want to give it to you."

"One more chance, young lady," he said sternly. "If I have to walk around the desk and take it from you myself, you will be one very sorry little girl."

Cheeks flushed a deep shade of pink, she passed him the journal and then jumped to her feet.

"Where do you think you're going?" he snapped, his agitation rising by the second.

She wrung her hands. "Oh, please, William. Must I really stay here while you read about what a big pervert I am? And anyway, I'm tired. I'd like to get ready for bed." Turning on her heels, she walked toward the door.

"Alexa Marie Benson, you will sit down right

now." The command in his voice reached her, and she shuffled back to her seat, burying her face in her hands as she sat down on the edge of the chair once again. "Good girl," he said.

His annoyance over her disobedience evaporated as he looked at the pink, glittery journal. Some of the sparkles rubbed off on his fingers as he opened it. Several days after their conversation on the front porch, when she'd confessed her new interest in age play, he'd given her the journal with instructions to write at least one new age play fantasy of hers each day. So far she hadn't complained about running out of ideas.

Flipping through the pages, he noticed the journal was already halfway filled up. Apparently she wasn't short on fantasies. He glanced up at Alexa and grinned when he saw her peeking at him through spread fingers. She quickly covered her face back up, as if embarrassed to be caught spying.

William turned to the first page. His cock immediately sprang to attention when he read the title of her fantasy: *Bath Time with Daddy*.

He read her bath time fantasy first, and kept reading straight through to the very last entry. As he became lost in her words, his mouth dried up and his desire heightened to the point his cock felt ready to burst through his pants. Her fantasies ranged from getting a spanking in the grocery store, to being punished for masturbating, to getting caught sneaking candy, to being in trouble for a bad report card, to snuggling on his lap while he read her a bedtime story. She also, to his immense delight, expressed an interest in dressing in frilly dresses, wearing her hair in pigtails, and donning stockings and girlish slippers. Shutting his eyes briefly, he visualized her in such an outfit, picturing her with a pouty face as she peered over her shoulder at him while in the corner with her naughty, well-punished bottom on display.

He closed the journal and placed it down on his desk. "Alexa, look at me." He waited until she lifted her eyes to his, her gorgeous blues clouded with worry. "You have nothing to be ashamed of. I'm rock hard right now and ready to explode after reading your journal. Thank you for sharing this with me," he said, tapping the journal.

"Truly?" Hope glimmered in her gaze.

He smiled. "Truly."

"Where do we go from here?" she asked nervously.

Leaning forward, he reached out until she placed one of her hands in his. He brushed his fingers atop the softness of her hand while he stared into her eyes. "We have the whole weekend just to ourselves, Lexie. You're going to be my sweet little girl, and I'm going to be your daddy. I'm in charge, and all you need to worry about is listening to your daddy. But first, we need to get you out of those grownup clothes. Stand up, little girl."

CHAPTER 3

Alexa trembled as William undressed her, and she hugged her center once he stripped off her last item of clothing—a black thong he said was not appropriate for his little girl to wear. Heat pulsed between her legs, and her eyes widened when she realized it wouldn't be long before moisture was trickling down her inner thighs.

"Lexie, uncross your arms right now, young lady. You aren't allowed to hide your body from Daddy," he scolded.

Heart racing, she dropped her arms to her sides. She shivered when he patted her bottom lightly, and as he circled her, she became increasingly aware of his authority over her. His hot breath tickled the back of her neck, and her skin prickled with each touch as he continued circling her, his eyes roving up and down her body. She flushed with shame, feeling hot all over as he continued his apparent inspection, lifting her breasts one at a time before moving to cup her bottom cheeks.

A gasp left her when he parted her cheeks, just long enough to expose her bottomhole and tap at her tight entrance twice before moving away, leaving her trembling with nervousness even as she ached for more of his attentions. He circled her again and knelt so his face was level with her pussy. As he reached for her smooth, intimate lips, she took two steps back and cupped her mound.

"Young lady, you will come here right now and let Daddy get a good look at you." Pointing at the floor, he indicated the exact spot where he expected her to stand. Authority radiated off him, and his frown of disapproval deepened when she shook her head.

"What are you doin', Daddy?" Feelings of embarrassment warred with her need to please William, her daddy.

"Inspecting my little girl," he said, again pointing at the floor.

She inhaled shakily and returned to the spot he'd indicated, her pussy tingling as he reached for her center once more. After he'd shaved her last week, he'd ordered her to keep her mound completely bare, even during the weekdays. The cool air drifted against her inner folds as he spread her lower lips, holding her open and paying special attention to her clit, which he tapped and blew against while she trembled in his hold. Finally, he released her and stood up. The sternness in his expression caused the air to leave her lungs.

"Lexie, I'm afraid you didn't do a very good job cleaning yourself the last time you took a bath."

Her heart lurched and threatened to beat out of her chest. "I-I'm sorry, Daddy."

"Don't worry, Daddy will take care of it. Come on, it's time for your bath, little girl." Grasping her hand, he led her from his office and to the huge master bathroom attached to their bedroom.

Alexa's breath hitched when he drew her close for a moment, kissing her forehead.

"Are you going to be Daddy's good little girl tonight, Lexie?" His warm hands cupped her bottom cheeks.

"Yes, Daddy."

As he gazed down at her, she became lost in his dark depths. The unmistakable bulge of his manhood poked at her through his pants, and her tummy fluttered. Daddy. He was going to take care of her tonight. All weekend, in fact. And he seemed just as excited about it as her.

"I'm not going to haul you over my knee for a proper spanking just yet, not for a few more weeks, Lexie." He touched the soft flesh beneath her left breast, where a faint yellowish bruise still marred her skin. She'd ceased wearing the wrap and thought she was mostly healed, but if she moved around too much or too quickly, a jolt of pain would shoot through her chest, reminding her that she wasn't fully recovered yet.

She grinned up at him, twirling a lock of hair between two fingers. "Does that mean I can get away with being naughty, Daddy?"

"Absolutely not, little girl. Naughtiness will be punished swiftly. If I think you need more than a few smacks to your bottom, I won't hesitate to reacquaint your bottomhole with the cane."

A shudder rippled through her. "I'll be a good girl, Daddy."

"I hope so." He rolled up his sleeves, smiled

encouragingly, and guided her toward the toilet. "Do you have to go potty, Lexie?"

Digging her feet in the cool tile floor, she shook her head and gazed at him wide-eyed. The idea of being completely taken care of had driven her wild with longing these past few weeks, but now that she was faced with one of the more embarrassing parts of her fantasies, she was overcome with shame and didn't think she could even sit down on the toilet in front of him, let alone relieve herself. It was far, far too humiliating. "No, Daddy, I'm fine!"

Ignoring her answer, he lifted the lid and pulled her forward despite her protests. "Be a good girl and go potty, Lexie. I know you haven't gone in a while."

She stomped her foot once and tried to twist out of his grasp. "I said I'm fine, Daddy!" Her face had never felt so hot, and she yelped as her daddy swatted the backs of her thighs. She danced around, trying to dodge the blows. It had been ages since she'd had a spanking, so her flesh was tender and unused to even the lightest smack. "Owie! No spankin', Daddy!"

"Little. Girls. Don't. Argue." He slapped her sit spots a dozen more times, bringing tears to her eyes.

Rising to his full height, he glowered down at her and held her out by the shoulders. "Are you going to listen to Daddy now?"

Blinking rapidly, she fought to hold her tears back, feeling foolish for resisting him so early on. Wasn't this what she wanted? Her lip trembled and she nodded. "Okay, Daddy. I'm sorry. Can you leave the bathroom at least?" She already knew his answer, but she couldn't help but try for a bit of privacy.

"No, little girl. Now sit down and go potty. Daddy really doesn't want to have to punish you again."

She obeyed, her face growing hotter as she relieved herself under Daddy's watchful gaze. She thought she'd never known shame so deep, but he added to her embarrassment moments later as he cleaned her up.

"Very good girl." Affection glimmered in his gorgeous eyes as he smiled at her.

She melted under his praise, though her shame didn't leave. She felt even more naked and exposed as she stood in the center of the bathroom while he prepared her bath. Excitement churned within her as she watched him add bubbles, and she smiled as he swirled his hand around in the water to make them grow.

"Okay, little girl," he said, standing up. "Let's get you in the bath tub." He picked her up as if she weighed nothing and placed her in the water.

Warmth surrounded her as she sank further into the tub, and she delighted in the bubbles surrounding her. She scooped up the bubbles and blew them out of her hands, giggling when a few hit Daddy in the face.

"Oops. Sorry, Daddy." Another giggle burst from her chest as he wiped the bubbles from his face with a towel. As she continued laughing and swishing her arms and legs around in the tub, water splattered over the edge and onto the floor.

"Little girl, you'd better calm down right now. No water on the floor."

She immediately stopped splashing and lowered her head. "I'm just havin' fun, Daddy," she mumbled, trying to restrain another smile. Even though he'd embarrassed her moments ago, and quite thoroughly, she suddenly felt playful. Of course it probably wasn't smart to test her daddy, not while she was naked and a bath brush hung on a rack nearby. Gulping, she looked at the bath brush and decided to settle down.

Daddy chuckled, following her gaze. He picked the heavy brush up and smacked it against his palm. "I almost forgot about this," he said, hitting his palm again. The heavy smacking sound made her jump. Once, almost a year ago, he'd paddled her with the terrible thing. A dozen spanks to her bottom cheeks and another dozen to her thighs.

Lexie gulped hard and remained absolutely still in the water. "Oh, Daddy, I'll be very good. Please don't spank me with the bath brush." The memory of the sting it packed made her bottom tingle and sent a jolt of fear through her center. Under no circumstances did she want a spanking with the bath brush, especially not with a wet bottom. She doubted Daddy would bother drying her off first should he have cause to punish her. She hoped to be a good girl and relief washed over her when he finally placed the brush aside.

He grabbed a washcloth and dipped it in the water, working up the bubbles in it before touching it to her breasts. Gasping, she closed her eyes for a second as a naughty thrill spiraled throughout her. Her nipples tightened as he soaped up her breasts, and her heart pounded when she opened her eyes to meet his affectionate gaze. He instructed her to lift her arms, and he continued bathing her while she sat pliantly and followed his instructions, for the most part.

"Daddy, that tickles!" she cried as he washed her feet. Unable to hold still, she kicked and tried to squirm away from the washcloth.

"Alexa Marie," he warned, grasping her ankles. "Be. Good."

She held her breath and closed her eyes until he finished with her feet, sighing in relief when he released her ankles. Finally. "You're a meanie, Daddy," she said, pouting, though a smile threatened to break through.

"If you think I'm a meanie now, just wait until I clean the rest of you." One dark, thick eyebrow rose up as he held her gaze while soaping up the washcloth again.

Shame filled her as the meaning of his words sank in.

"Lay back in the tub and spread your legs, little girl. Daddy needs to wash your privates." He held the washcloth up and looked at her expectantly.

"Yes, Daddy," she said, feeling her nipples tingle and burn at his calm command. She was so aroused she was practically panting, and she flushed knowing her daddy would see the evidence of her excitement. Surely her clit was noticeably swollen. Though the water would shield her moisture, everything below her waist ached and throbbed. She leaned back in the tub and parted her thighs, whimpering as he pushed the bubbles away to reveal her sex.

"Hmm," he said. "I want a better look at you." Pulling the plug, he didn't replace it until the tub had drained to leave only an inch of water beneath her.

Peering down at her body, Alexa's face heated when she realized her bare folds were on display for her daddy. His gaze was dark, but a tenderness also reflected in his eyes as he looked upon her.

"You're beautiful, little girl." He reached between her legs with the soapy washcloth and began to clean her, taking his time.

Alexa resisted the urge to buck her hips and meet his hand as he parted her slick folds. Swollen and dark pink, her clit throbbed with need as Daddy worked the cloth around her privates, but avoided her nub, much to her frustration.

"Spread those legs wider, Lexie."

She obeyed, and a thrill rippled through her when he pressed one finger to her bottomhole, thrusting the tip in and out while she whimpered and shuddered with pleasure. The sound of her quick, moaning gasps filled the bathroom as he continued, delving deeper and deeper into her tightness, and eventually adding a second finger.

"Daddy has to make sure you're all clean," he said, his voice gravelly. The desire was evident in his eyes, and knowing he was enjoying giving her a bath heightened Alexa's delight.

Finally, he reached between her legs with his other hand and touched her clit. She jerked in response, her head falling back as pleasure consumed her. Circling her stiffened nub with his thumb, he drew moisture from her core and the soap suds overtop her pulsing clit.

"I know you're all achy down here, Lexie, and I want you to relax and let go right now. Be a good girl and come for Daddy."

Her release descended upon her in an avalanche of sensation. Pressing her center against his hand, she cried out as he pumped harder and deeper into her bottomhole, filling her up completely while she rode the waves of pleasure flowing throughout her body. Her toes curled and her hands formed into fists.

"That's it, Lexie. Good girl."

As the last pulsing remnants of her orgasm faded, her daddy removed his fingers from her bottom, slowly withdrawing them before rubbing the washcloth over her sensitive folds once more. Whimpering, she remained still with her legs spread while he finished cleaning her.

The warm regard in his gaze when she looked up stole her breath away.

WILLIAM WRAPPED A FLUFFY WHITE TOWEL AROUND Alexa and helped her out of the tub. He'd rinsed her off and decided bath time was over. She hadn't protested, and she fought to suppress a yawn as he gathered her close. A surge of protectiveness for his little wife rose in his chest. She was so sweet and adorable, and he drew her closer and kissed the top of her head, wishing their special weekend would never end.

He had many activities planned, some of them fantasies she'd written about in her journal, and others that were his idea entirely. He hoped she liked what he'd planned, and he hoped the shared experience would bring them closer. Her trust and love was a gift he cherished, as was her submission, and he vowed to take good care of his sweet little Lexie.

"Let's get you ready for bed and then Daddy will read you a story. How does that sound, Lexie?"

She peered up at him shyly from under her thick lashes, but her eyes held a brightness that betrayed her excitement, and she soon broke into a smile. "Really, Daddy?" she asked hopefully.

He chuckled. "Yes really, little girl. Now come on, let's go into your bedroom."

Confusion spread across her face when he led her back through the master bedroom and out into the hallway.

"Where are we going, Daddy?"

"To your bedroom."

"But…" Her voice trailed off when he opened the guest bedroom door to reveal her new little girl room.

"This," he said, guiding her inside, "will be your room on weekends."

He glanced at her, gauging her reaction as she scanned the room with wide eyes. A small gasp left her and her lips parted. She squeezed his hand and he led her farther inside, holding his breath and waiting for her to share her thoughts. He'd spent his free time working on it during the last week, an hour here and an hour there, during the times Alexa happened to be out of the house. Boxes filled with the items he needed for her room had arrived nearly every day, and he'd ordered her not to open anything while he was at work, under threat of another bottomhole caning.

"You did all this for me, Daddy?" She released his hand and spun in a circle, gazing at the walls adorned with paintings of butterflies, princesses, and fairies. Longing flickered across her face as she gazed at the huge rocking chair and the bookcase, filled with new books, of course. A giggle escaped her as she touched the pink bedspread, and she grinned at the stuffed animals resting atop her pillow.

William strode to the closet and opened it. "Daddy will dress you each morning and get you ready for bed each night on the weekends, Lexie."

"Oh, Daddy, this is wonderful!" Clutching the towel still wrapped around her, she rushed to his side and peered into the closet, which was filled with girlish dresses and outfits.

"Do you like your room?" he asked, swallowing hard.

"I love it!" She bounced up and down and threw her arms around him, and her towel dropped to the floor, leaving her naked body pressing against his.

Pink stained her cheeks when he pulled back to gaze into her soft blue eyes, and she tried to bend down and grasp the towel, but he seized her wrists and forced her to stand encased in his arms for a lingering embrace. "All right, Lexie." He released her from the hug and walked to the dresser. "Let's get you in some jammies. Come here, little girl."

Her blush deepened and she kept her head lowered as she approached him. Opening the top drawer, he retrieved a pair of cotton, floral patterned panties. Thank God for the Internet and priority shipping. He'd worried the clothing items he'd ordered wouldn't arrive in time, but luckily they'd showed up yesterday afternoon. Just in time to add to his little girl's new room. The boxes that had arrived today contained more stuffed animals and a few more dresses.

"Step in," William said, bending down as he held the panties open.

Alexa wobbled as she stepped into her panties and grabbed onto his shoulders for balance. After slipping the panties over her hips, he patted her bottom and stood up, turning back to the dresser. From the second drawer he withdrew a pair of pink, drop seat pajamas. He couldn't wait to see her wearing them and anticipated giving her a demonstration of just how handy the drop seat was when it came to maintaining discipline.

"In you go," he said, kneeling again and holding the legs out while she stepped inside. With great care, he pulled the pajamas up and over her body and zipped up the front once her arms filled out the sleeves.

"Thank you, Daddy," she whispered, cupping her bottom and peering over her shoulder, obviously curious about the flap that could be opened to expose her bottom.

A heated longing gripped William, and his cock swelled as his desire escalated with each second as he watched Alexa inspecting her pajamas. He visualized her toppled over his knee with the drop seat hanging open while he spanked her soundly for misbehaving, and later making her stand in the corner with her naughty red bottom sticking out, the flap hanging open beneath her freshly punished cheeks. He also imagined her embarrassment as he unsnapped the drop seat and sat her on the potty before bedtime, urging her to be a good girl and refusing to leave the room even as she blushed with shame while relieving herself in his presence.

"Lexie," he said, standing her directly before him, "you've been a very good girl today, but I'm going to give you a demonstration right now so you know what to expect if you're naughty for Daddy." Guiding her to the bed, he stood her between his legs and stared up at her, drinking in her beautiful, feminine features.

His cock stirred again at the idea of turning her bottom cheeks pink with a gentle spanking, just hard enough to sting and remind her that he was the daddy and she was the little girl. He'd be careful and loving as he turned her backside a pretty shade of pink. He'd told her he didn't plan to give her a proper spanking until her rib healed, and he intended to keep that promise, but he knew she was aching for a taste of his discipline. Aside from the bottomhole caning and a few swats here and there, it had been weeks since she'd experienced a chastisement at his hand.

"Are you gonna spank me, Daddy?" she asked softly, worry transpiring on her face. She fidgeted in place and twisted her hands together.

"Yes, little girl. Just a tiny spanking though. A dozen quick smacks as long as you cooperate. Can you do that? Can you be my good girl, Lexie?"

"Yes, Daddy, I'll be a good girl."

He smiled, then slowly guided her across his lap, positioning her body so her legs and chest rested on the bed. Pausing with a hand on her bottom, he listened for any signs of distress. Her breathing was heavy, but she didn't appear to be in any pain.

"How are you doing, little one?" he asked. "Is this position okay for you?"

"Yes, Daddy," she said, wiggling her bottom slightly as if impatient to get her spanking started.

William was only too happy to oblige.

He cupped her bottom for a moment before working the buttons of her drop seat open, one by one as her breathing became more labored. She peered back at him with large blue eyes that gave her an air of innocence. Silken waves of hair fell across her face, and she turned around and tensed her bottom cheeks, shifting overtop William's lap and causing his hardness to swell painfully against her center.

"Now," he said, using his sternest daddy-voice, "Daddy expects you to be on your best behavior this weekend, Lexie." He finished unsnapping the last button and pulled the drop seat down, revealing her cute little panty-clad bottom. Touching the soft cotton of her flower patterned underwear, he cupped her backside briefly before tugging the panties down to rest beneath her bottom cheeks. A sigh of satisfaction left him, and he caressed her nakedness while she remained still over his lap, being a very good girl for her daddy.

"I promise I'll be on my bestest, most goodest behavior, Daddy," she replied, once again wiggling her butt and arching into his caressing hand.

"You must obey Daddy at all times, Lexie. You must ask permission to do anything, including going outside, going to the potty, watching television, or getting a snack. Is this understood?"

"Yes, Daddy, I understand."

"Good. Also, your bedtime will be nine o'clock."

She jolted on his lap. "What? Daddy that's so early! Please can I stay up until eleven? Or at least ten?"

"Absolutely not. Keep arguing and I'll make it eight o'clock."

Silence filled the room as she rested her head on the bedspread, seeming to accept his rule.

"Time for your spanking, little girl." He tightened his hold on her waist. "You'll be in skirts, dresses, or drop seat jammies all weekend long, every weekend, so Daddy has immediate access to your bottom. Keep that in mind before you get up to any mischief."

He raised his hand and brought it down with a crack just hard enough to leave pinkness coloring her flesh. Applying the remaining eleven spanks to her bottom, he spread the smacks out over her cheeks, and he was pleased at the color her backside had turned under his hand.

"All right, little girl. You took your spanking well." Massaging her freshly spanked mounds, he cupped each cheek and let his fingers wander near her crevice, teasing her tight bottom entrance as a reminder of the other types of punishment he might mete out if she were naughty.

Turning her over on his lap, he cuddled her against his chest, delighting in the way her naked bottom pressed against his center. His cock throbbed with the need to have her, but he had other plans for Lexie tonight.

"It's getting late. Let's finish getting you ready for bed, little girl, then Daddy will read you a story and get you all tucked in. Okay?"

She peered up at him with eyes full of adoration. The look of love made his throat tighten, and he smoothed her hair out of her face, thankful that she'd shared her desire to explore age play with him. She grinned and snuggled deeper into his chest before rising to her feet with his help. The flap of her drop seat swayed beneath her bare little bottom as she moved. "Okay, Daddy," she finally answered. "Even though I still think nine o'clock is way too early a bedtime. Ouch! Owie! No more spankin', Daddy. I'll be good!"

CHAPTER 4

Alexa didn't particularly enjoy going potty in front of Daddy again, or allowing him to help brush her teeth, but she did enjoy the bedtime story and sitting on his lap in the rocking chair. She couldn't believe he'd sneaked around in between his busy work schedule last week to arrange her new room. The constant flow of packages, many of them huge, over the past few days had aroused her suspicions, but she hadn't suspected a gesture this grand. She felt loved and cherished beyond measure.

"One more story, Daddy? Please?"

"Okay, little girl. Just one more. But then I expect you to go straight to sleep." He selected a book she thought was much too young for her, a short rhyming book about fish.

She opened her mouth, ready to voice her displeasure, but the faint stinging of her bottom reminded her that Daddy could be stern. She really didn't want to earn a punishment. Closing her mouth, she settled further into his lap and listened as he began the story. To her delight, he read the rhymes in a playful tone that made her giggle and actually enjoy the book. Well, it wasn't really the book she enjoyed. It was the special time with Daddy. She sighed against his chest after the story ended, then suppressed a yawn.

Daddy rubbed her back and rocked her for a few minutes, holding her close as she drifted off. In fact, she fell asleep in his arms and didn't even realize it until she awoke briefly as he tucked her into bed, moving the stuffed animals aside to make space for her. His lips brushed across her forehead, and she tried to wake up enough to say goodnight, but fatigue pulled her back into the thick fog of sleep, making speech difficult.

"Goodnight, Lexie, my sweet little girl."

ALEXA AWOKE THE NEXT MORNING AS THE RISING sun streamed through the sheer white curtains. She stretched and yawned, then sat up rubbing her eyes and trying to wake up. Gazing at her surroundings, her heart pounded with excitement. Last night with Daddy had been wonderful and she couldn't wait to see what experiences today held. She bounced out of bed and hurried to her closet, selecting a pink frilly dress with white petticoats underneath it. It reminded her of a tutu. But a second later, she hung the dress back up, remembering Daddy had said he would dress her each morning. Her bottom tingled and warmth pulsed between her thighs at the thought of what might happen if she disobeyed. Backing away from the closet, she grabbed a book about a singing princess and hopped back into bed.

Minutes passed and she became engrossed in the book, and she hugged a teddy bear to her chest as she read. The floorboards creaking in the hallway alerted her to Daddy's approach, and she slammed the book shut and grinned as the door opened.

"Mornin', Daddy!" She bounded off the bed and nearly knocked him over with her tackle hug.

"I see someone got up on the right side of the bed." His chuckle rumbled next to her ear as he swept her up in his arms. "Are you hungry?"

"A little," she said, then a terrible thought struck

her. "Um, Daddy, am I allowed to have coffee?" Alexa doubted she'd be able to survive through the morning without it.

"Absolutely not. Little girls aren't allowed to have coffee, Lexie." He ruffled her hair as she frowned up at him.

After taking her to the potty, Daddy led her downstairs and fixed her a bowl of oatmeal with fresh strawberries. While oatmeal wasn't her favorite food, she ate it anyway without a fuss, but she didn't touch the glass of milk he'd placed in front of her. Nope. No way was she drinking that icky stuff. She hated milk and only tolerated it if heaps of chocolate were mixed in.

"Young lady," Daddy said, peering at her from over his newspaper, "You need to be a good girl and finish your milk."

"But it's so yucky, Daddy." She pouted. "Could I have chocolate in it?"

He shook his head. "Too much sugar, Lexie. You'd be bouncing off the walls. Now drink your milk all gone and then you can watch some cartoons while Daddy takes a shower."

Alexa glared at the glass of milk while her daddy continued reading his newspaper and sipping at his coffee. The smell of it wafted in her direction and made her all the angrier. It wasn't fair. Crossing her arms, she let her legs swing back and forth under the table and refused to touch the milk.

Daddy folded his newspaper and pushed it aside, then leaned forward to stare directly into her eyes, giving her *the look*. Anxiety twisted her stomach and she hurriedly reached for the glass. Well, fine. She'd drink it. She supposed it was better than getting a sore bottom, or even worse—a sore bottomhole.

Wrinkling her nose, she took a sip, making noises of displeasure after she swallowed the vile liquid. "Oh please, Daddy, don't make me drink it. Just a little coffee? Please? I'll die without it."

"Stop being a little drama queen, Lexie, and drink your milk. Now."

She huffed and scowled at him, but picked the glass up again and took another sip. And another sip. She drank the whole thing slowly, keeping her nose wrinkled the entire time. Once it was emptied, she pushed the glass away and avoided Daddy's gaze.

"I thought you woke up on the right side of the bed, little one," he said, standing to collect the dirty dishes. "Keep it up with the bad attitude and you'll earn yourself an early bedtime tonight. I won't stand for a grumpy little girl."

Inhaling quickly, she sat up straighter and stared at him in alarm. Nine o'clock was early enough. "I'm sorry, Daddy. I'll be good."

"I thought so."

After taking her to the potty again and helping her brush her teeth, Daddy got her settled on the couch with her teddy bear and flipped through the stations until he found some cartoons. A weight of worries Alexa hadn't even realized she'd been carrying lifted from her shoulders. She snuggled under the warm fleece blanket Daddy had placed on her lap and stared at the television, suddenly captivated by Wile E. Coyote chasing the Road Runner toward a cliff.

The sound of the shower running drifted down from upstairs, and Alexa stifled a yawn. She was still upset about the milk and lack of coffee, but she supposed William wouldn't be a very good daddy if he let her have her way all the time. And besides that, what kind of daddy let his little girl drink coffee anyway?

She smiled as she thought about how stern he'd been with her in the kitchen, peering at her over his newspaper with a no-nonsense look. She squirmed as electric warmth traveled to her center, but she resisted touching herself. Maybe if she was a good girl Daddy would give her another bubble bath and stroke her swollen nub until pleasure shot through her in waves again. She pushed the blanket away, suddenly hot.

Wanting Daddy to find her where he'd left her on the couch, she hugged her teddy bear to her chest and curled against a pillow, her attention back on the cartoon. A sense of déjà vu descended upon her as she continued watching; she thought back to her childhood and Saturday mornings spent watching cartoons. Of course her parents were usually both working and she was home alone, often sitting at the coffee table in front of the television with a bowl of cold cereal she'd fixed herself. It wasn't until she was a teenager that they began working less, after her father had a heart attack and realized he needed to slow down, and her mother had decided to cut back on work hours to help him recover.

Glancing up the steps, she smiled. She wasn't alone right now, and she'd never feel alone again. It wasn't that her parents had been bad parents. She still loved them and had a decent relationship with them, but each time she thought of her childhood, memories of long, lonely weekends spent at home came rushing back. As a kid, she'd always been jealous of her friends whose parents didn't work so much, and she'd been especially jealous of her friends who had lots of siblings.

The shower cut off and Alexa's thoughts returned to Daddy. Snuggling on his lap while he read her stories had felt intimate on a level she'd never experienced. She'd felt so safe nestled in his arms, his deep voice reverberating against her ear. William, Daddy, had a tender, nurturing side that she loved and wanted to experience more of. He also had a stern side, and she pressed her legs together as an ache built as she imagined going over his knee for a long, hard spanking.

A real punishment spanking while she was his little girl on the weekend.

She wondered how different it would feel compared to the spankings she received as a grownup on the occasions she was naughty.

Footsteps sounded on the stairs, and Daddy returned to cuddle her on the couch, smelling like his woodsy, manly soap and aftershave. She nestled her cheek against his freshly shaven one and sighed contentedly as she inhaled his scent. His hair was still damp from the shower, and she delighted in sculpting it into a Mohawk before slumping back down on the couch. Amusement flickered in Daddy's dark eyes, and a smile tugged at his lips as he stared down at her. She laughed.

"Little girl, you'd better fix it right now or you'll be getting a close up view of the carpet."

A thrill rolled through her tummy at his playful threat. Giggling, she sat up and smoothed his hair back into place. "Oh fine, Daddy. There. All fixed, your royal highness."

He tipped her chin up, forcing her to meet his gaze. Though some of the playfulness remained in his eyes, a hint of seriousness also glimmered in his dark depths. She swallowed hard, wondering if she was in trouble. Maybe she had been too argumentative during breakfast and now Daddy was going to punish her tight bottomhole again. Her backside clenched involuntarily, and moisture started to gather in her panties.

"I want to have a fun day with you, little girl. We're going to get you dressed, then run a few errands before coming back home for the rest of the day. I expect you to be on your best behavior, young lady."

Her mouth suddenly dry, Alexa only managed a nod. When he raised an eyebrow at her and continued to stare, she gulped and licked her lips, struggling to find her voice. "Okay, Daddy."

"All right then, let's go get you out of these jammies and into a cute little dress."

"THESE PANTIES ARE SOAKED, LEXIE. ARE YOU SURE you didn't have an accident?" William ran a hand between her thighs again, detecting her immense moisture through the thin cotton underwear.

"Daddy, please!" She covered her face and shuddered. "You're embarrassin' me. No, I didn't have an accident!"

He towered over her and pried her hands from her flushed face. "Then why is your underwear so wet, young lady?"

"Please don't make me tell you, Daddy." She tried to cover her face again, but he grasped her wrists and pinned her arms at her sides.

"If you didn't have an accident, then you must have been entertaining some very unladylike thoughts while I was in the shower. Did you touch yourself, little girl? I certainly hope not. You know that sort of thing is against the rules." He used his most scolding tone and watched as a new blush stained Lexie's cheeks. Little gasps left her as she peered up at him, wide-eyed and completely and utterly embarrassed.

"Daddy, I didn't touch myself! I swear it. Cross my heart and everything." Panic reflected in her eyes, and she squirmed in place as he maintained a hold on her wrists.

William pulled her hands up and smelled them for signs of her arousal. If she'd touched herself, the odor would be pungent on her fingers, but he didn't detect the slightest trace of her feminine essence coating her fingertips. "I believe you, Lexie," he said, watching her visibly relax at his pronouncement.

"Thank you, Daddy."

He stepped away, leaving Lexie standing in the center of her room, only wearing the pair of wet panties and with the pajamas still bunched around her ankles. After selecting a pink dress that was sticking out from the other hanging clothes, likely because Lexie had been looking at it, he grabbed a pair of sparkly pink slippers and turned to find his little girl still blushing profusely.

"Before I get you dressed, young lady, I need to clean your privates thoroughly." He paused, watching her eyes grow even wider. "You made quite the mess."

He placed the dress on the bed and the shoes beside it on the floor, and hurried Lexie to the bathroom, swatting her bottom a few times and scolding her for having impure thoughts and making such a mess in her panties. She shuffled along beside him, moving her legs quickly to keep up, the pajamas still tangled around her ankles. Once they entered the bathroom, he helped her step out of the jammies and wet panties, and ordered her to sit on the edge of the tub with her legs parted wide.

Shaking his head, he stared at her glistening center. "If this keeps happening, Lexie, I will start putting you in a diaper. A big thick diaper that will stick out from underneath your dresses. Is that what you want?"

A shuddering gasp escaped through her lips and she cupped her wet center, shaking her head. "Please don't do that, Daddy. I would be so embarrassed!"

William stared at her for several moments, letting his threat hang in the air. When they'd been discussing her desires, she'd said she didn't wish to go little enough to be put into diapers, but that didn't mean he wouldn't threaten it, if only to watch her blush the darkest shade of pink he'd ever seen coloring her face. She didn't need to tell him she was embarrassed, it was more than obvious.

"Uncover yourself, Lexie."

Biting her lip, she stared at him for several seconds, unmoving, before finally removing her hand from between her legs. Glistening and pretty pink, her pussy was once again displayed to him. He grabbed a fresh washcloth and ran warm water over it.

"I can clean myself, Daddy," Lexie said as he knelt between her spread thighs. She clutched the side of the tub, her legs trembling as the occasional whimper left her throat. Her nipples were erect, and goose bumps covered her arms and legs.

William pressed the warm, wet cloth to her privates and began cleansing the moisture from her smooth folds. "Daddy is happy to take care it, Lexie," he said, softening his voice. "I'm proud of you for not touching yourself, but I'd be interested to know what kind of thoughts you were having. You were supposed to be watching cartoons."

"I was watchin' cartoons."

"Tell Daddy about the naughty thoughts that led you to wet your panties." He finished wiping her folds and pressed a dry towel to her intimate parts.

"I-I was thinkin' about what it might be like to be spanked, you know, to get a real punishment spankin', as your little girl."

Smirking, William met her gaze. "And were you planning on a specific sort of naughtiness to earn such a spanking?"

She shook her head, and her sleep-mussed hair became even more disheveled with her movements. "No, Daddy, I'm plannin' on bein' a good girl for you. Honest."

He smiled and gathered up the towel, tossing it into the hamper along with her underwear and jammies. Reaching a hand toward her, he waited until she accepted it and hauled her up, kissing her forehead and holding her in the circle of his arms.

"All right. Time to get you dressed for the day." William guided her back to the bedroom and helped her step into a pair of panties first, then slipped the dress he'd laid out earlier over her head, taking his time as he pulled it down over her curves.

Lexie looked adorable wearing the pink frilly dress. As she twirled around her bedroom, allowing the petticoats to flare outward with her antics and occasionally revealing her plain white panties, he retrieved a pair of white, knee high stockings. Once he got her to stand still for a minute, he slipped them on her feet and drew them up her calves. The sparkly pink slippers completed her outfit, and he surveyed her with approval before grabbing a hairbrush and two ribbons off her dresser.

"Come sit on the floor right here." He sank down in the rocking chair and pointed at the rug beneath his spread legs.

"Okay, Daddy." She flounced over and sat cross-legged on the floor, tilting her head back and sighing as he began brushing out her tangled locks.

William parted her hair into high pigtails, holding each side up with a pink ribbon tied in a bow. Once satisfied with the girlish style, he patted her on the head and urged her to stand.

"Let's go run those errands, little girl. You can be Daddy's special helper."

Nervousness filled her features as she peered at him over her shoulder, blinking back at him with worry. "What kind of errands, Daddy? Are we goin' inside any stores?"

"I need to drop some letters off at the post office, fill the car up with gas, and pick up a few items from Andy's Hardware. You can stay in the car during our first two stops, but you will be accompanying me inside the hardware store. I might be a while and I can't leave a little girl like yourself unattended for that long. I hope that won't be a problem, Lexie." His folded his arms across his chest, waiting for her response.

She chewed on her lower lip and turned to face him, then lowered her head to stare at her sparkling slippers. "Can I stay home and watch cartoons, Daddy? Please?"

"Absolutely not."

Her head shot up and she stomped her foot on the floor. "But I don't wanna leave the house, Daddy!" She stuck out her lip and glared up at him sullenly.

Uncrossing his arms, his jaw clenched and he stabbed a finger in her direction. Disappointment surged through him. He expected her to trust him enough not to embarrass her in public. They lived in a small town and he certainly didn't want to give anyone a reason to talk badly about her. Which was why he'd picked Andy's Hardware. His friend had agreed to allow them inside the store during the hour he closed for lunch. Only Andy, and possibly his wife, Tina, would be present. They were all close friends and had even gone on vacation together a few times. There had been plenty of times the other couple had heard Alexa getting her naughty bottom paddled, and likewise there had been plenty of times William and Alexa had overheard Tina getting spanked by Andy.

"Alexa Marie, I'm going to count to three. If you don't turn around and start walking to the car, you'll be one sorry little girl, I promise you that."

She harrumphed and her glare hardened, her eyes becoming slits of icy rage. He could tell she was wavering on the edge of a full blown temper tantrum. Despite how naughty she was being, he thought she looked cute standing there in the middle of her room, wearing the girlish outfit while sulking up a storm. Her adorableness wouldn't save her from suffering the consequences of misbehavior though.

"One. Two. Three."

Alexa still hadn't moved an inch.

CHAPTER 5

"No, Daddy, please don't put that in my bottom!" Alexa struggled to rise up from the bed, but Daddy easily held her firmly in place, bent over with her naked bottom exposed. After she'd refused to leave the house, he'd raised the layers of her skirt and given her a few quick, hard swats. Then he'd made her stand in the corner with her dress hiked up around her waist and her panties tangled around her ankles. She'd thought that brief but stingy spanking had been all he'd planned.

But she'd thought wrong.

During her corner time, Daddy had retrieved a bottle of lube and a butt plug from their bedroom.

"Lexie, this is for your own good. I want to make sure you behave today. Having a plug in your bottom will no doubt remind you to be a good girl." His voice was gentle, contrasting with the firm hold he maintained on her.

Taking a deep breath, Alexa attempted to calm herself. Tears burned in her eyes. She'd wanted to stay home all day with Daddy. Going out in public, especially dressed so childishly, struck fear into her heart. Besides that, she was still reeling from his threat to put her in diapers if she kept dampening her panties with her arousal. To her complete mortification, that threat had excited her in unexpected ways, causing her nipples to tighten and longing to pulse through her center. She closed her eyes and breathed in and out, slowly, reminding herself that she trusted Daddy.

"Okay, Daddy. I'm sorry."

"That's my good girl. Now relax that little bottomhole of yours and let Daddy inside."

Cool liquid was drizzled down her crevice, and he began pumping the lubrication in and out of her tightness with a finger. She remained bent over the bed, clutching the covers as heat scorched her face. No matter how many times he'd attended to her bottomhole before, being spread wide open never failed to fill her with humiliation. She held her breath as he pushed the plug past her tight resistance, and gasped for air the moment it was fully seated in her bottom.

"Very good girl, Lexie." He patted her sore butt, helped her to stand, and pulled up her panties.

Unable to look Daddy in the eye, Alexa concentrated on smoothing her skirts out and fixing her disheveled hair.

"All right, Lexie, let's go." He clasped her hand and guided her outside.

The sun streamed down from a cloudless blue sky, and Alexa smiled when she noticed the red tulips had finally blossomed in the flowerbeds lining their walkway. The familiar scent of the fresh blooms filled her with joy. Spring was her favorite season by far, and as she gazed around the neighborhood, she smiled to see the cherry blossom buds ready to burst open. Perhaps in a few days the street would be lined with gorgeous trees in full bloom. Daddy guided her to his car, pulling her from her thoughts of flowers and blooming trees.

She was shocked to discover he expected her to sit in the backseat, but warmth spread through her chest as he buckled her in and kissed her cheek before closing the door. He drove to the post office first and deposited a short stack of envelopes into the big blue mailbox in front of the building. Next, they traveled to the gas station, and she fidgeted in the back seat and looked around the parking lot as Daddy filled his car up. Even though no one in the lot could see her, it was exciting and liberating to be out of the house dressed in her new little girl clothes.

The hardware store was their next stop though. Her heart pounded. Daddy expected her to accompany him inside, and her face heated at the thought of someone seeing her walking around the store, holding her daddy's hand. What would people think? She was still shocked he'd brought her out in public, but she pushed her worries away and decided to trust him. Somehow, it would work out.

On the drive to Andy's Hardware, Alexa toyed with the white petticoats underneath her dress. Her stomach flipped the moment Daddy pulled into the hardware store parking lot, and she scanned the area, ready to count the cars so she had an idea of how many people might be inside. To her confusion, she only saw Andy's blue truck.

She squinted and leaned closer to the window, staring at the store entrance. A large sign hanging on the front door read "Gone to Lunch."

Of course! She felt silly as it all clicked into place. Andy closed down his store between eleven o'clock and noon for lunch each day. It was a small store and he ran it with Tina, and Alexa didn't have to worry about bumping into anyone but her two friends. She nearly started bouncing up and down in the backseat.

Excitement churned within her, and the same moisture that had gotten her in trouble earlier gathered in her panties, warm and wet against her smooth lips. What would Daddy say if he discovered her wetness? Would he really make her wear diapers like a baby?

"Daddy just needs to pick up a few things at the store, Lexie," he said as he parked near Andy's truck.

Seconds later, he was opening her door and unfastening her seatbelt. Alexa wasn't sure if she could contain her excitement. The urge to grasp Daddy's hand and hurry him into the store fell upon her, but she managed some self-control and followed his lead, walking at his steady pace. He knocked on the door, and Andy appeared with a key in hand. Once it was open, Alexa followed Daddy inside and nervously glanced at Andy.

"Thanks for letting us in," Daddy said to his friend.

"It's my pleasure." Andy turned to Alexa.

"You're looking very pretty in your dress today, Lexie. I hope you're being a good girl today." He closed and locked the door, but kept his gaze on her, apparently waiting for a response.

"Um…" Oh no. Her voice had abandoned her. She swallowed hard and stared at her feet.

"Lexie, he just paid you a very nice comple-ment. What do you say?" Displeasure rumbled in Daddy's deep voice.

Lexie. Andy had called her Lexie too. She looked at Daddy suddenly, and her pigtails flipped about her head with her rapid movements. She wondered how much Daddy had told his friend, but quickly decided it didn't matter.

She swallowed hard again, determined to find her elusive voice. "Th-thank you, Andy."

Daddy stiffened. "Alexa Marie, you know very well you're not allowed to call Andy by his first name. He's an adult and you're a little girl. I ought to lift your skirts up and paddle your bottom red right now."

She gasped and looked from Daddy to Andy. "I-I'm sorry, Mr. Ridland. Thank you for the compliment."

"Apology accepted, Lexie," Andy said, moving toward the checkout counter.

Daddy relaxed his shoulders, and Alexa breathed a sigh of relief. She scanned the store, looking for Tina. Apparently reading her thoughts, Andy leaned across the counter and said, "Tina is home sick today."

Alexa nodded and walked beside Daddy as he moved down the aisles, perusing the tools and gardening supplies. Whatever he was looking for, it was taking forever for him to find it. Boredom soon filled her as they ventured down yet another aisle. Daddy released her hand and knelt to inspect a tool kit of some sort on the bottom shelf, and Alexa backed up a few steps, needing a change of scenery.

"Daddy, I'm so bored!" she declared, stomping her foot.

He frowned up at her, still holding the tool kit. "Lexie, do I need to take you back out to the car?"

She gulped at his warning. She was pretty sure what would happen if he had to take her back to the car. A spanking. She most certainly didn't want a spanking, especially in the parking lot.

"Sorry, Daddy. I'll be quiet."

His concentration returned to the tool kit, but Alexa found it hard to stand still and keep quiet as promised. Maybe she should go for a walk. Of course Daddy probably wouldn't allow it, but she wouldn't go far. She would even return by the time he finished in this aisle and her brief absence would go unnoticed.

Creeping to the end of the aisle, she glanced at Daddy to find him still busy reading the back of the small tool kit. The lines on his forehead were creased in concentration. She spent a moment admiring how handsome he looked today. His hair appeared mussed, even though he'd washed and combed it this morning. When he went too long in between haircuts, his locks, though short, became as unruly as hers in the morning. Her fingers itched with the desire to rake through his hair, but she paused halfway to him.

He was concentrating awfully hard on the back of that darned tool kit. She frowned and crossed her arms, feeling sullen that he was taking so long in the hardware store. Standing at the end of the aisle, she tried to be a good girl and wait patiently, but her adventurous spirit soon got the best of her.

Alexa escaped around the end of the aisle. Once out of his vision, should he look up from the tool kit, she paused and waited to hear her name.

The silence indicated he hadn't noticed her absence. She grinned, feeling her boredom slip away. She had a whole store to explore and she didn't have to follow Daddy around and keep stopping every two seconds to stare at an item. That was even worse than sitting in the car while Daddy ran errands. It was Saturday and she decided weekends were meant for fun, not for boring grownup stuff.

She skipped down an aisle filled with how-to books, her petticoats bouncing underneath her skirt. Halfway down the aisle, she noticed a bright orange sale sign hanging from the ceiling. She jumped, stretching her arms above her in an attempt to touch the bottom of it. No luck. She gazed up at the sign, suddenly determined to jump high enough to touch the sign and make it swing from the ceiling. Slipping her shoes off, she kicked them aside and stood beneath the sign again. *One, two, three…*

She jumped again, but her fingers didn't come close to grazing the sign, and upon landing she stumbled into a display of gardening books. The display toppled over with a crash, the books spilling to the floor. It was at that moment she spotted Daddy standing at the end of the aisle, his face a mask of worry and anger.

William couldn't believe Lexie had wandered off, let alone made such a mess in the store. He approached her as she scrambled to right the display and place the last of the fallen books back into place. She paused and gazed up at him fearfully when his shadow fell upon her.

"Where are your shoes?" he snapped.

From her spot on the floor, she pointed across the aisle. He fetched her slippers and knelt to place them on her feet, then pulled her up to stand in front of him. He'd been worried to discover her missing from his side. Now that he'd found her, apparently up to no good, agitation bubbled hot underneath his surface.

"I'm sorry, Daddy!" she cried. "I didn't mean to knock the books over. It was an accident."

He grasped her upper arms and leveled a stern look on her. "Young lady, you knew you weren't to wander off. Why did you walk away from Daddy?"

Biting her lip, she peered up at him with unshed tears glistening in her eyes. "I-I was bored is all. Then I was jumpin', tryin' to touch that sign," she said, gesturing to a sale sign that hung high up on the ceiling, much too high for a little girl to reach. "I didn't mean to knock over the books."

"Alexa Marie Benson, you were very naughty."

He positioned her at his side and forced her to bend forward.

"Oh, Daddy, please no! No spankin'! Someone might see!"

"You should have thought about that before you were so naughty. Now keep still."

He started spanking overtop her dress, warming her bottom with a series of quick swats. Then, flipping her skirt and all the layers of her petticoats up, he slapped her panty-clad bottom while she squirmed and whimpered.

"Daddy, please don't lift my skirt up!"

Ignoring her protests, he swatted her bottom a few more times before yanking her underwear down to rest at her knees.

"Daddy, noooooo!"

"Panties come down for all your spankings, Lexie. It doesn't matter where we are. Naughty little girls always get spanked on their bare bottoms."

As she continued struggling, he caught sight of the butt plug seated between her cheeks. Apparently it hadn't been enough to ensure her good behavior. He should have given her a harder spanking before leaving the house today. Once he determined her backside was a sufficient shade of dark pink, he yanked her underwear back up and smoothed her skirts into place as he brought her upright.

Holding her out by her shoulders, he said, "Now we're going to check out and then go home. When we get home, you're going to stand in the corner with your little red butt on display."

She sniffled and wiped at her tears. He hadn't spanked her too hard and he wouldn't be able to for another few weeks, and he suspected it was remorse and embarrassment that had caused her tears to fall. Staring up at him, she rubbed her backside and nodded. "Okay, Daddy. I really am sorry."

William led her back through the aisles, selecting a few gardening items and a set of wrenches before heading for the counter. Lexie kept pace with him and didn't try to wander off again. Occasionally she rubbed her bottom or wiped at her eyes. Once they reached the front counter and Andy began ringing up the items, she remained a few steps behind him, her head lowered.

"Is everything all right, Lexie?" Andy asked as he handed William the large bag containing all his purchases.

"She's probably not in a talking mood," William explained. "Miss Lexie wandered off and got herself into a little bit of trouble in your store, I'm afraid."

"Is that so?" Andy asked. "I thought I heard a commotion earlier. It sounded like a little girl was being taken to task."

"Yes, she got a spanking on her bare bottom for wandering off and getting into some mischief, didn't you, Lexie?"

Her head shot up and she peered at them in shock, her cheeks flushing the same dark shade of pink as her bottom. Tucking a strand of hair behind her ear, she glanced at the floor in her embarrassment. "Yes, I got a spankin'," she said in a low, childish voice.

William thanked Andy for his help and guided his little girl to the car. She was quiet during the drive, and once they arrived home, he marched her to her bedroom for corner time. She stood with her nose to the wall obediently, her dress raised up, and her panties around her ankles. William admired her cute bottom, still reddened from her recent spanking, and sat on her bed watching to ensure she stayed put. After ten minutes, he called her out of the corner and wrapped his arms around her, soothing her pain with soft words of forgiveness.

Lexie hugged him tight and her sniffling soon

ceased. He smiled down at her and kissed her forehead, and his heart rejoiced when she returned his smile. She'd been naughty, but he'd punished her and now it was over, and all was right between them again.

The rest of the weekend passed quickly. William enjoyed taking care of all of Lexie's needs and anticipated their next daddy/little girl weekend together. He bathed her again on Saturday night, read her several stories, and tucked her in with her stuffed animals as he'd done the evening before. On Sunday he promised she could sleep with him as long as she took a nap, and though she grumbled that she wasn't sleepy, she drifted off not long after being tucked in and slept for two straight hours. He awoke her shortly before dinner time, brushing the hair from her face and stroking her cheek until her blue eyes fluttered open.

"Hi, Daddy," she said through a yawn. She blinked up at him and smiled.

"Hi, sleepyhead. How would you like to help Daddy set the table?"

Lexie nodded with enthusiasm and jumped out of bed. After dinner and her shower, she put on her big girl pajamas and joined him on the couch. He snuggled her for a few minutes, tucking her under the fleece blanket she always curled up with while watching cartoons.

"Alexa," he said, turning the television off. "I want to talk to you about this weekend."

She stiffened.

"It's nothing bad, sweetie. Please relax. I enjoyed this weekend very much."

Sighing, she relaxed in his arms. Relief shone in her eyes as she gazed up at him. "You promise?"

"Of course, sweetie. I want to do this next weekend too, and the weekend after that, and so on." Pressing a kiss to her forehead, his lips lingered as he inhaled the scent of her lavender body wash. He could hold her like this every day, all day. Alexa was the best thing to ever happen to him, and he'd thought their relationship was damn near perfect before she'd brought up age play. But somehow, in one short weekend, he felt closer to her than he'd ever felt before. And God, how he wanted her. He ached for her with his entire being.

"I'm so relieved, William." Her eyes widened for a moment. "Can I call you William now? I wasn't sure, um, how to end this."

"How about we transition back to regular ol' boring William and Alexa each Sunday after dinner? You can take a shower and put your grownup pajamas on, and then join me in bed."

Grinning, she toyed with the buttons on his shirt. "Oh please. We aren't boring. But I like that idea. I started to feel like my usual self as I took a shower and dressed myself. I think it will work."

William leaned down to kiss her, but paused when he noticed half of the buttons on his shirt were undone. Sitting back, he glared down at her with mock sternness. "Young lady, this conversation isn't quite over."

Lust darkened her eyes and she unfastened another button. "Perhaps we can move it into the bedroom then?"

Imprisoning her wrists, he held her captive in his lap. "There's one more thing I'd like to discuss with you, and you must be completely honest with me, Alexa. Even if it embarrasses you."

Alarm flashed briefly in her gaze, but she nodded and waited for him to continue.

"I know you said you didn't want to go very young, Alexa. You specifically said you had no interest in diapers and being bottle fed. I respect that and don't want to force you into going younger than you wish. However, sweetie, the thought of seeing you wearing a diaper appeals to me greatly, and I discovered your underwear soaking wet on a few occasions this weekend. Perhaps," he said, releasing her hands to cup her face, "we can try diapering next time."

To his relief, she didn't make a face or cringe away from him. His heart was pounding so fast he was certain she must hear it. It thumped in his ears, the echo growing louder with each second as he awaited her response.

Alexa's head tilted to the side and she looked at him quizzically. "I can't believe I was worried about telling you I wanted to try age play." She straightened and met his gaze, the lust returning to her eyes. "I'm not opposed to wearing them. But not for their intended purpose, if you catch my meaning."

"I understand, and if you decide it makes you too uncomfortable, we won't do it next time."

She squirmed on his lap, grinding against his rock hard erection. "That sounds good to me. Can we go to the bedroom now?"

William chuckled and scooped her up, carrying her to their room. "By the time I've had my fill of you, Alexa, I doubt you'll be able to sit comfortably at your new job tomorrow."

"Is that so?"

He entered their bedroom and laid her on the

bed, a primal urge coursing through him as his balls tensed and his cock swelled further, pressing tight against his jeans. Crawling atop Alexa, he pinned her hands down and leaned to growl into her ear. "Yes it is. You'll be lucky if you can walk straight tomorrow too. Now, let's see what's under these pajamas of yours."

ALEXA TREMBLED WITH DESIRE AND PARTED HER thighs, arching her center toward William as he settled his weight upon her. His bare skin felt heated against hers, and she let her hands wander up and down his arms, enjoying the feel of his solid muscles beneath her fingers. Pleasure quaked through her when he latched onto one nipple, sucking and pulling it with his teeth. Each tug of her sensitive peak tightened the ball of pleasure in her lower tummy, prompting her to writhe beneath him. She groaned at the delicious sensations and gasped when he released her breast, only to pay the same attention to her other nipple, sucking and drawing his teeth along the taut peak.

"I need you now," Alexa said, almost begging. Moist warmth gathered in her inner core and escaped to rub against his cock, but he didn't press inside, leaving her frustrated and longing to be filled up by his hugeness.

"All in good time," he said, now trailing kisses along her neck.

She gave an irritated growl and once again pressed her center against his stiff length, but her impatience only earned her four sharp swats to the fronts of her thighs, two on each side. The sting of the unexpected slaps had her gasping again, but she managed to still her body beneath his in accordance with his wishes.

He grinned against her mouth and kissed her deeply, his tongue delving between her lips as he took command of the kiss, before pulling away to stare down at her with lust smoldering in his dark eyes. She was hungry for more of his kisses and caresses, even though her center continued to pulse with a deep need that wouldn't be quenched until he plunged into her.

"You're beautiful, Alexa," he said, grasping one breast and toying with her nipple, driving her mad with more tugs that sent jolts of sensation straight to her aching pussy.

"And you're the meanest husband I've ever had." She narrowed her eyes and scowled as best she could as he tormented her most sensitive spots. Her nipples. The side of her neck. Her earlobe. And the bit of flesh between her pussy lips and her bottomhole. He teased her with his hands, his mouth, and his teeth, throwing her into a frenzy of longing and leaving her breathless.

Pressing her eyes shut, she tilted on the verge of shamelessly begging him to claim her. The smell of her arousal filled the air and mingled with William's masculine, woodsy scent. Sweat trickled down her temple, her entire body heated from the passion flaring between them. She'd been waiting for this moment all weekend. Did he really have to torment her so?

"Meanest husband ever," she muttered.

Hot breath fanned against her neck as he put his lips to her ear. "I can be meaner, if you'd like." Splaying her slick folds apart, he delved between her pussy lips and spread moisture from her center over her pulsing clit.

Alexa circled her arms around his neck and cried out, bucking into his hand and quivering as an orgasm approached. Just as she thought it was about to descend upon her in a glorious wave, he removed his hand and left her bereft of his touch.

"You're a monster!" she cried, hitting at his chest.

William easily captured her wrists and held her arms above her head in one hand. With his free hand, he groped her breasts and lazily trailed his fingertips across her stomach, before moving lower once again. "And you, my little sweetie, are in need of a lesson in manners. You've been trying to order me around in bed since the moment I took your clothes off. Yes, a strict lesson in manners is exactly what you need, little wife." He swatted her pussy, and the sound of the single slap reverberated through the room.

She stared at him as the shock of the abrupt smack faded, along with the sting, and tried to close her thighs. It was no use. He positioned his body atop her legs, preventing her movement, and struck her intimate folds again. Alexa gasped with each crack of his hand over her pulsing, aching flesh. The sound of wet slaps rang out steadily, and she had no choice but to lay there and accept her punishment. William scolded her as he spanked her pussy, telling her he expected her obedience in the bedroom just as he did outside of it.

Her chest heaved with her gasping breaths, and she watched with wide eyes as he continued to bring his hand down, again and again over her smooth pussy lips. Finally, he stopped spanking, and slid two fingers through her folds and then held them up in the air. Her moisture glistened on his fingers.

"Do you see this, young lady? This is why I'm going to put you in diapers next weekend, Alexa." His tone was stern, but his gaze was heated. His words shamed her deeply, and she longed to cover her face, but his hold on her wrists remained firm.

After tormenting her clit for several more minutes, swirling her wet arousal over it only to pull away just before she came, he flipped her over on her hands and knees and pulled her hips up. She shivered with pleasure and arched her bottom up to meet his entrance. The air left her when he slammed into her pussy, filling her up with his cock at last. He stilled within her tightness for a moment before withdrawing all the way only to surge inside again. Over and over. It was pure bliss, and all thoughts fled from her mind as he pounded into her, bringing her closer to the sweet peak of her release.

Reaching underneath her, he stroked and pinched her clit, not missing a beat as he fucked her so hard the headboard banged against the wall. As William's strokes became faster, his body tensed, and as he began to groan and fill her up with his seed, she fell into the abyss of a relief sweeter than she'd ever known. Before he withdrew from her pussy, her muscles contracted around his length, pulsing with the remnants of her orgasm. She peered over her shoulder at William, trying to catch her breath. Sweat glistened on his sculpted arms and broad chest, and his gentle smile warmed her heart.

She collapsed underneath him and closed her eyes, certain that they'd never been closer and their marriage more intact than in this moment. Suddenly, she was in his arms, and she sighed against his chest, marveling at how the time they'd spent as Daddy and Lexie had carried over into the adult side of their relationship, deepening their intimacy and strengthening the bonds of their love.

CHAPTER 6

"What's all this?" William cupped Lexie's moist center, detecting the wetness of her arousal through her cotton panties. "I asked you a question, young lady."

"Please don't make me tell you, Daddy." She peered at him from behind her spread fingers, and the instant he met her gaze she covered her face to hide her shame.

William sighed deeply and stood up. "This is your second pair of panties today, Lexie. You keep getting them wet. Are you having naughty thoughts again?"

She remained still and kept silent. Of course she knew what was coming. They'd discussed it the weekend prior, and he'd warned her what to expect if she failed to keep her panties dry.

"Lexie, look at me."

Reluctantly, she met his gaze, looking up at him with her pigtails in disarray from her nap. "Daddy, I'm so embarrassed." Red infused her cheeks as she stared into his eyes.

The layers of her pink dress bounced back into place as William stepped away. He'd put her in a dress similar to the one she'd worn last Saturday, except it was slightly shorter and contained more petticoats underneath. He suspected the bulk of a diaper would lift her dress farther up and reveal the bottom of the diaper as she walked, or at least whenever she bent over. White knee high socks and a pair of black Mary-Janes completed her outfit, and he took a few seconds to admire how adorable she looked today.

"Lexie, I'm afraid I have no choice but to put you in a diaper now." He retrieved the diaper bag he'd assembled from beside the dresser and pulled out the plastic changing mat. Unfolding it, he laid it on the floor and beckoned Lexie to come forward.

At first, she didn't move. William patted the changing mat and infused his voice with warmth. "Lie down right here, little one, Daddy's got to get that diaper on you. Be a good girl and lift your legs up too."

"Okay, Daddy," she said after a deep, shuddering breath. Alexa obeyed, laying on the mat with her knees bent slightly and her feet planted on the floor.

"Lift those legs up, young lady. If you don't cooperate, Daddy will have to spank you first. Do you want a spanking, little girl?"

She whimpered. "No spankin', Daddy." The petticoats of her short dress fell back as she acquiesced to his command, raising her legs like a good girl.

Touching the wetness soaking her panties, he waited until she met his gaze with those gorgeous blue eyes of hers. Though her cheeks were still reddened with embarrassment, her ever increasing breathing testified to her arousal, and he swore her panties grew even damper as he stared at her and lightly caressed her privates though the thin cotton.

"Keep very still," he said when she began to squirm. He slipped a finger inside her underwear and traced a circle around her swollen clit. "Daddy needs to see how wet you are, Lexie."

Instead of arguing or groaning in frustration as he half-expected she would, she lifted her legs higher and pulled her thighs apart, giving him better access. William drew her panties up to her knees, needing to see her smooth pink folds. He splayed her lips apart to inspect her arousal further. Throughout his inspection, he left no fold or tiny crevice untouched.

"You're positively soaking, little girl. We'd better get this diaper on your cute little bottom right now before you make a mess on the changing mat."

As he expected, his words caused another flush of embarrassment to redden her face. William removed her panties and reminded her to hold position with her legs high in the air while he cleaned her folds with a baby wipe. He pulled a diaper from the bag and slid it under her bottom as he lifted Lexie up by her ankles. Retrieving the baby powder, he twisted the lid open and sprinkled a generous amount atop her folds, then rubbed the white substance into her skin with great care. He took his time and enjoyed every little gasp and noise Lexie made.

"You're being a very good girl for Daddy," he said, his voice full of praise.

William closed the diaper up, fastening the sides and leaning back to admire his handiwork. To his surprise, Lexie's body shook with a sudden giggle as she returned her feet to the floor. She peered through her spread legs at him and covered her mouth as another giggle escaped, her pigtails bouncing with her laughter.

He raised an eyebrow at her. "And just what's so funny, young lady?"

Uncovering her mouth, she sat up on her elbows and her smile vanished. Unease crept across her features, and she gnawed at her bottom lip as she continued to regard him through her spread thighs. "Well, Daddy," she finally said, "I was just thinkin' that I could get away with being naughty when I have a diaper on." Another giggle. "I don't think it'll hurt much if you spank me."

"First of all, Lexie, if you're especially naughty, Daddy will take your diaper off and then spank your bare bottom. Second of all, if I spank you over your diaper, you will still feel the sting. And if you don't, Daddy will spank the backs of your thighs instead." Coming to kneel at her side, he urged her to lay back down on the changing mat. "And as a matter of fact, I think you need a bit of a demon-stration, Lexie."

"Wh-what? Daddy, no! I was just kiddin' around!"

William clasped her ankles together and set into

her diaper-clad bottom, striking her backside with quick swats that had her face twisting in pain after the first dozen.

"Okay, Daddy. I get it. You don't have to—"

He cut her off with a series of slaps to the backs of her thighs that really got her attention. She attempted to twist out of his grasp, but he held onto her ankles and continued spanking her thighs until her flesh turned dark pink. A few more swats to her bottom over her diaper, and William finally released her legs and helped her to stand. With her head lowered, she stood before him submissively and reached around to rub her backside. He tipped her chin up and forced her to meet his gaze.

"Well, Lexie, what do you think? Do spankings still hurt when you have a diaper on?"

Her lips parted and she gawked at him with wide eyes, then nodded and tried to pull her chin from his grasp. William cupped her face in both hands, not allowing her to look away. Desire wound up tight within him to see her so nervous to answer one simple question. "Well?" he prompted.

"Y-yes, Daddy. Spankin's still hurt when I have a diaper on."

William hugged her and then made her stand in the center of her bedroom while he circled her, inspecting her appearance from head to toe. Her pigtails cascaded over her shoulders. Today he'd braided them and tied the ends with a ribbon. Baby soft wisps of hair had escaped the braids in a few places, and he tucked the errand strands behind her ears. Next, he knelt to pull up one of her knee-high socks that had fallen down during her struggles. After rising to his feet, he walked behind Lexie and gazed at her bottom. The diaper he'd chosen was so bulky and large on her tiny butt that it visibly poked out of her short dress, the hint of white contrasting with the lacy pink layers of her dress.

"Let's go over the rules before we continue with our day, Lexie. Come sit on Daddy's lap."

He led her to the rocking chair, sat down, and patted his thigh. She crawled on his lap and curled up against his chest, resting her head directly over his heart. As he rocked her and snuggled her, brushing those baby soft strands of hair behind her ears again, she gazed up at him with a peaceful, trusting expression of pure contentment.

"I love you, Daddy." She toyed with the buttons on his shirt and continued to stare at him from under her thick, dark eyelashes.

Emotion swelled within him and his throat tightened as he regarded his sweet little girl. He loved her more every day, if that were possible, the affection he felt for Lexie swelling eternally in his heart. "I love you too, Lexie." He pressed a soft kiss to each of her cheeks, then an even softer kiss to her lips. She shuddered and wrapped her arms around him, wiggling on his lap enticingly.

He pulled away and stilled her movements with a stern look. "Little girl, are you trying to distract Daddy from our discussion?"

"Oh, Daddy, don't be silly," she said with mock innocence. "I'm just sitting on your lap like a good girl."

He tapped her nose playfully, twice. "No more squirming. Now, about those rules. You still need to ask for permission to go potty, especially since Daddy will have to take your diaper off first. You are also forbidden to take your diaper off yourself. If I catch you doing that, I'll put a plug in your bottomhole before putting a new diaper on you. Understood?"

She sighed and cupped the side of his face, her fingertips dancing over his stubble. "Yes, Daddy, I understand."

"Good girl."

They enjoyed each other's company for the rest of the weekend, and Lexie was on her best behavior

—mostly. Aside from a few swats with the bath brush for splashing water on the floor during bath time, she didn't incur another spanking. William kept her in diapers the entire time, finding he loved the look of her nappy poking out from under her dresses. She became more accustomed to wearing them, and after a few more weekends came and went, she admitted to looking forward to being diapered by him first thing on Friday evenings.

William insisted she visit the doctor to check on her rib one last time, so he scheduled her an appointment exactly eight weeks after her accident. He took the day off work to bring her to the appointment, and her continued protests that she could drive herself earned her the promise of a hard, bare bottom spanking once the doctor confirmed she was healthy and healed.

On the day of the appointment, she rolled over in bed and covered her head with a pillow when he tried to wake her up.

"Go away, William! I am still sleeping!"

Annoyance flared hot under his skin, and William decided he'd had enough of her naughtiness. She not only kept insisting she could go to her appointment alone, but she even suggested she didn't need to go to the appointment in the first place and might as well cancel it. Well, he'd had enough of her tantrums. Tossing the covers back, he yanked her panties down and started spanking her bottom cheeks, hard.

"Ouch! Owie! Stop it." She wiggled on the bed and threw her pillow to the floor, her little legs drumming against the mattress as he reddened her backside.

"I've had enough of your tantrums, Lexie," he said, intentionally using her little name. "Now you be a good girl and get your naughty bottom out of bed this instant, or Daddy is going to spread your cheeks and punish your bottomhole. Do you want Daddy to get the cane?"

ALEXA DIDN'T WANT DADDY TO GET THE CANE. HER mind spun. She hadn't thought he'd want her to be little for her doctor's appointment. It was Friday, but she'd assumed they would begin their usual daddy/little weekend after they got home. Her bottom stung, and panic skittered through her when she remembered the purpose of today's appointment. Daddy wanted to make sure her rib was all healed, and because she'd been grumpy and fussed about her impending appointment, even after he'd warned her to stop several times, he'd promised her a real punishment spanking once the doctor verified her full recovery.

Her tummy flipped, and she cried out as Daddy spread her cheeks and pressed a finger against her bottomhole. She clenched her butt, but it didn't deter his exploration.

"Lexie, I want you to be a good girl today, but if I need to give you a more severe punishment before we leave for the doctor's office, I won't hesitate to bend you over the bed and cane your bottomhole."

Whimpering, she tried to relax as he pressed inside her tightness, filling her up with his finger. Without lubrication, the intrusion burned and she struggled to remain still while he thrust in and out. "Please, Daddy, not the cane. I promise I'll be good." The worries about her appointment faded and she began to feel silly for having resisted Daddy. He had good intentions and only wanted to make sure she had fully recovered. She didn't particularly like going to the doctor though, and she'd been angry when he'd made the appointment without first consulting her.

Daddy pumped into her bottom a few more times before withdrawing and turning her over. Her panties tangled around her knees, and the sheets irritated her sore backside. And it hadn't even been a real punishment spanking! She stared at her daddy's chest as remorse welled up inside her and combined with her fear over the proper spanking he'd promised her. Would it happen today? Tomorrow? Though she wanted to know for certain, she couldn't bring herself to ask. Instead, she lifted her eyes to his and took a deep breath.

"I'm really sorry I've been fighting you over the appointment, Daddy. I just don't think I need to go." She pushed at the spot on her chest that had once been the source of a piercing pain so great it brought tears to her eyes. Now the bruises had faded and she didn't feel the slightest bit of soreness, even when she pressed hard against it. "See, Daddy? I'm allllllll healed."

"I'm glad it doesn't hurt anymore, Lexie, but you're still going to the doctor. If you're a good girl at your appointment, Daddy will take you out for an ice cream cone on the way home. How does that sound?" He smiled and stroked her thigh. She'd slept in nothing but a T-shirt and a pair of panties, but she decided to always wear pajamas from now on. The more layers between her bottom and Daddy's firm hand, the better.

She considered his offer and grinned. "Can I get vanilla with rainbow sprinkles?"

He chuckled. "Yes, little girl. Whatever you want." He patted her thigh. "Now get up. We have to hurry."

Since they were going out in public, Daddy permitted Alexa to wear one of her grownup dresses. He selected a pink, knee-length dress with white polka dots, and even though it was an older dress and currently out of fashion, she didn't put up a fuss. He did, however, insist she wear a pair of her little girl panties, as well as white stockings and sparkly pink slippers. He allowed her to wear her hair down, but promised to braid it into pigtails with ribbons after they returned home. She spun in front of her mirror once and decided she was happy with her appearance. After a quick breakfast of cinnamon raisin bagels and yucky milk, Daddy drove her to her appointment across town.

Not only did Dr. Stevens give Alexa a clean bill of health, but they were in and out of his office in thirty minutes. She was relieved to have the dreaded appointment over so quickly, and she bounced up and down in the back seat after they left, continuously reminding Daddy that she wanted rainbow sprinkles on her ice cream cone. He ordered her a

kiddie size cone, complete with the requested sprinkles, and she finished the whole thing by the time
they arrived home.

Daddy opened her door and unbuckled her,
and she climbed out of the back seat with his
help. A perfumed breeze swept down from the
flowering trees, and she thought he looked quite
handsome with the wind ruffling his hair, the lines
around his dark eyes crinkling as he squinted in
the sun. She swallowed hard, knowing that at any
moment he could march her to her room and
turn her over his knee. She repressed a shudder
and her eyes grew wide as she felt moisture in her
panties.

"You look worried." He shut the car door and
guided her to the house. "Tell Daddy what's wrong,
little one."

Her mind raced for a response. She didn't want
to mention the punishment spanking yet. Now that
she thought about it, he hadn't mentioned it yet
today either. Maybe it was her lucky day and he'd
come down with temporary amnesia. She certainly
didn't want to put any ideas into his head by
bringing it up first.

"Lexie," he warned. "What is it?" They entered
the house and he shut the door, turning her to face

him as he locked it. Two firm hands came to rest upon her shoulders.

"Um, well, Daddy…" *Think think think.* She felt another trickle of moisture escape her privates, soaking her panties further. It was the answer to her dilemma. She lowered her head, shame heating her cheeks. "My panties are very wet, Daddy."

He tipped her chin up, and she met his amused eyes. "I'm sure they are, Lexie." He shook his head. "I should have put a diaper on you before we left the house."

Her face flamed at the idea of wearing a diaper in public, and another surge of wetness coated her underwear. She was so embarrassed she wanted to hide from Daddy, but at the same time she wanted him to take care of her. No one else in the world loved her as unconditionally as Daddy, and she loved him in return with her heart and soul and everything she had inside her. His gaze roved up and down her body, lingering at her chest. She glanced down and realized her nipples were hard and visible through her bra and dress.

"I know your panties are probably soaked right now, Lexie, and I will be putting a diaper on your cute little bottom very soon, but there's another matter I must attend to first."

Alexa didn't like the sound of that. Her lip quivered and she instinctively cupped her backside. "Oh please, Daddy, no spankin'."

"After all the temper tantrums you've had over one doctor's appointment, you, little girl, have earned yourself a long, hard spanking. One that is well overdue, in my opinion."

He released her chin and she tried to shrink away, but he clasped her hand and led her upstairs to her bedroom. She hadn't been inside it since Sunday afternoon, and she glanced around at the room that always made her feel safe and loved. The colorful decorations always reminded her of how much Daddy cared about her, and her eyes blurred with tears up as she stared at the stuffed animals on her bed.

Daddy drew her close and hugged her, stroking her hair and giving her the reassurance of his love that she so desperately needed in this moment. She wrapped her arms around him and shuddered, wishing the embrace could last forever. But no. She'd been a naughty girl and her daddy had to punish her. Closing her eyes, she recalled how argumentative she'd been of late and remorse brimmed in her heart.

"I'm sorry I was so naughty, Daddy."

"I know you are, little one, but Daddy still has to spank you." His deep voice rumbled next to her ear. "I care about your health and safety very much. If you try to get out of a doctor's appointment in the future, especially if you argue with Daddy over and over again about it, you can expect there to be severe consequences."

She sighed against his chest and mourned the loss of his warmth when he pulled away.

"It's time," he said, moving to the bed. Sinking down on the mattress, he patted his thigh and gave her an expectant look. "Over Daddy's knee, little one. Let's get your spanking over with."

Lexie bit her lip to still its quivering and crawled over his lap. He situated her over one knee and brought his other leg atop hers. Her mouth went dry and her heart skipped a beat when he flipped the layers of her skirt up. Tugging her stockings and panties down, he tightened his hold on her and cupped her bare bottom. His touch sent a shiver through her. She braced herself for the first smack, hoping her punishment would be over quickly, though in her heart she knew she deserved the long spanking he had promised.

Much too soon, he began her punishment.

Daddy swatted Alexa's bottom, peppering both

her cheeks with sharp, rapid slaps. After about a dozen, she reached back to shield her backside, but he pinned her hands at the small of her back and continued striking her already tender flesh. It had been months since she'd gotten a real punishment spanking, and her bottom wasn't used to the intensity of his swats. Tears streamed down her face as the pain built, and she squirmed and thrashed over his lap, unable to hold still.

"Owie! Please stop, Daddy!"

Ignoring her pleas, he pelted the backs of her thighs. When the pain became unbearable, his hand mercifully moved higher to swat her bottom again, the fresh volley of smacks reigniting her already scorching flesh. She sobbed into the covers, gasping for air in between her cries. His hand kept falling, and she didn't think the spanking would ever end.

"Please, Daddy!" Her voice sounded hoarse and her throat burned from the emotion welling within her. She was sorry she'd been so naughty, especially after he'd taken such good care of her after the accident.

"It was a simple follow-up appointment, Lexie, and you spent the last two weeks stomping your foot over it and giving Daddy a hard time. I'm going to make all your doctor's appointments for you in the future and take you to them myself, and I expect you to behave like the sweet little girl I know you are." The pace of his spanks increased, causing Alexa to howl and squirm in a desperate attempt to escape the blows.

When he finally stopped, she cried over his lap while he rubbed her tender bottom. The light spankings he'd given her during the last few weekends didn't hold a candle to this punishment. Her shoulders shook as she released her emotion, hoping Daddy would forgive her for being so difficult, but his next words caused her sobs to deepen.

"Lexie, I want you to place two pillows in the center of the bed and lay over them."

Ice water flowed through her veins and her stomach dropped to the floor. She'd hoped the spanking was over and longed to be enclosed in her daddy's strong, forgiving embrace. She sniffled as she crawled off his lap and moved to comply with his command, arranging the pillows in the center of the bed. The stockings and underwear resting above her knees slowed her progress, and she paused before taking up the position on the pillows, not wishing to find out what else Daddy had planned. Her insides quivered when he stood up and began removing his belt.

"You need to lie down over the pillows, little one."

She cupped her sore bottom through her dress and stared at the pillows as if they would bite her. A raised eyebrow from Daddy had her rushing to comply though, and she climbed over the pillows and remained still as he lifted her dress, exposing her tender backside. She clutched the covers beneath her and held her breath, listening for the sound of his folded belt whooshing through the air. She knew she'd hear it before feeling the terrible sting.

Sure enough, she detected the whooshing noise and buried her face in the bed, crying out at the moment of impact. The first few strikes fell across the center of her backside, the thick leather lashing both her cheeks. Sobs racked her body, and it took all her self-control to stay in place over the pillows when the belt crashed upon her upper thighs. She was thankful he hadn't ordered her to count.

The lashes moved upward again and Daddy brought the belt down across her quivering bottom cheeks. She covered her face and winced with each blow. Each strike hit her like a lash of fire, over and over again as Daddy continued to mete out her punishment. She'd be reminded of this spanking each time she sat down for days and days.

The belt ceased falling and a gentle hand touched her shoulder. The bed dipped with Daddy's weight as he sat next to her, and she peered up at him with tears streaming down her face, seeking the kindness and forgiveness she always saw in his gaze after a punishment. The look of love and concern in his eyes made her cry harder.

"Shh, little one. Your spanking is over." He caressed her sore bottom and lifted her up in his lap, cradling her on the bed while whispering words of forgiveness in her ear. She latched onto him as her tears gradually dried up, thankful that her punishment had ended.

Daddy smelled like aftershave and laundry detergent, and she found the combination soothing as she nestled her face in the crook of his arm. He pressed a tissue to her cheeks, drying the last of her tears, and melted her with his kind smile.

"Come on, Lexie." He patted her leg. "Let's get your diaper on and then we'll cuddle some more in the rocking chair."

Alexa obediently laid on the changing mat and lifted her legs as Daddy removed her stockings and underwear. He cleaned the arousal from her privates with a baby wipe and placed a diaper beneath her bottom. Next, he sprinkled powder on her center, rubbing it into her skin with slow caresses. A sense of peace descended upon her as she gazed up him, watching as he tended to her with great care.

After he closed up her diaper, he lifted her and carried her to the rocking chair. She loved sitting on his lap in the rocking chair, even if her bottom was sore. Once seated, he cradled her in his arms and stared at her with a tenderness that made her heart dance with joy.

The sound of rain pattering on the roof prompted Alexa to glance out the window at the dark sky. She didn't mind the bad weather though. She'd spend the whole day with Daddy inside, and that was fine with her.

"How about after lunch we watch a movie?"

She grinned, excitement swirling through her. Watching a movie meant lots of snuggle time with Daddy under a warm blanket on the couch. She couldn't think of a better way to spend the after-noon. "That sounds great, Daddy. Um, can we watch Beauty and the Beast?"

"Are you sure that's not too scary?"

She blew an errant strand of hair out of her

face and gave him a mock pout. "It's not scary at all, Daddy! Please can we watch it?"

He stroked her cheek and kissed her forehead. "All right, little one. Beauty and the Beast it is. I'll even make popcorn."

"Oh, thank you, Daddy!"

The rain fell harder, beating a trancelike rhythm on the roof as Daddy rocked Lexie. Her eyes began to feel heavy, and she fought to stay alert, not wanting to spend a minute of her special weekend with Daddy asleep, unless he was making her take a nap or go to bed for the night. As his comforting presence permeated her senses, she blinked up at him and suppressed a yawn. There was nowhere else in the universe she'd rather be than in her daddy's strong, loving arms. He kissed her forehead again, and the heat of his lips lingered as he straightened to gaze into her eyes.

"Daddy loves you very much, little one. You'll always be my sweet little Lexie."

ABOUT SUE LYNDON

USA TODAY BESTSELLING AUTHOR SUE LYNDON writes naughty, heartfelt romance filled with sexy discipline, breathless surrender, and scorching hot passion. Hard alpha males, strict husbands, fierce alien warriors, and stern daddy-doms make her go weak in the knees. She's a #1 Amazon bestseller in multiple categories, including Sci-Fi Romance, Historical Romance, BDSM Erotica, and Fantasy Romance. She also writes vanilla sci-fi romance under the name Sue Mercury —but no matter the genre or pen name, her books always have a swoon-worthy happily ever after.

WWW.SUELYNDON.COM

Get FREE reads when you sign up for Sue's newsletter—and be the first to hear about freebies, sales, and new releases:

https://www.suelyndon.com/newsletter-sign-up